NETS AND LIES

By Katie Ashley

Love + hugs
Katie
Ashley

Cover Image: Shutterstock
Cover Design: Letitia Hasser at RBA Designs

Chapter One: *Melanie*

A crisp swoosh echoed over the gymnasium just as the final buzzer rang. The crowd erupted in a roar as they clamored to their feet. I barely had time to wipe the salty sting of sweat from my blue eyes before my teammates pounced on me in a dizzying flurry of back slapping and hugging. "Way to go, Mel!" they screamed. Their voices were almost engulfed by the cheering crowd.

My face stretched into a wide grin as my mind and body got swept away by the wave of their excitement. A hand on my shoulder caused me to whirl around. It was Coach Thompson, or Coach T as we affectionately referred to him.

"That's my girl!" he cried, crushing me to him in an appreciative hug.

I couldn't fight the warmth spreading over my cheeks when his arms lingered on me, keeping me flush against his body. I never liked being the center of attention. I was the epitome of "There's No I in Team", so I didn't like being singled out. "Thanks," I finally mumbled.

He winked at me and then turned to the others. "All right, let's do our run through to the other team and then meet me back in the locker room!"

We obediently lined up to high-five the losing team and mutter the obligatory "Good game" line. Many of them glared at me since my foul shots had sent us over the edge to win. As I jogged over to the locker room, my own personal cheering section, my parents and grandparents, swished blue and white pompoms and hollered my name. I grinned up at them and waved.

The Varsity boys' team lined up to take to the court. Before I could make it into the locker-room, my boyfriend, Will, swept me into a bear hug and then planted a lingering kiss on my lips. "Whoa, get a room, Thompson!" one of his teammates shouted while some others whistled.

"Will," I protested, as my hands pushed against his chest.

"What?"

I blushed. "I'm all sweaty and gross."

He grinned. "I like you all sweaty and gross. It's *sexy*!"

My heartbeat accelerated as I ducked my head. "Whatever."

"All right, all right, Will. Get your hands off my star and get your head on the game!" Coach T bellowed.

Will's hands jerked from my waist like he had been scalded by Coach T's words. "Jeez, Dad, I was only congratulating her."

Cocking his head, Coach T eyed Will sternly. "Maybe if you had a bit more discipline, you'd bust your ass like Melanie."

My cheeks burned in embarrassment for Will. Coach T was always so hard on him—too hard for my liking. Will was a gifted athlete, but he would never be perfect enough in his father's eyes. Then again, it always seemed like whenever I was around, Coach T reigned down even harder on Will.

Will scowled as Coach T stalked by us and threw open his office door. I tentatively put my hand on

4

Will's shoulder. "Hey, good luck out there." Then I leaned over and kissed him.

When I pulled away, he smiled. "Thanks, beautiful," he said, as he playfully tugged on my sweat-slickened ponytail. "Go get a shower and then come cheer me on."

I nodded and headed into the athletic offices. I'd just gotten through the door when I heard Coach T consoling Amanda Weathers. Backed up against the wall of his office with her head bowed, she was sobbing over the two shots she had missed. Coach T didn't take mistakes lightly, even when we were victorious, but he always tried to comfort us when felt we had failed the team and ourselves.

Amanda raised her head long enough to shoot me an embarrassed look as I breezed past her. I hurried down the corridor to the locker-room. When I headed inside, I found it teeming with JV and Varsity players, emptying their lockers and getting changed.

After quickly shedding my sweat-soaked uniform, I stepped into the shower. Steaming hot water scalded my body, causing me to moan in a mixture of pleasure and pain. Muscles constricted and screamed in agony at their overuse. I guess you could say I was a firm believer in the "Play Hard or Go Home" mantra.

As I lathered the long strands of my blonde hair, I heard laughter next to me. "Was that a moan for Mr. Hot Stuff?" my best friend, Lauren, asked.

I rolled my eyes. "No, it wasn't."

Lauren shot me a wicked look. "You're wasting a prime opportunity there, Mel. He has to be one of the hottest guys in school, not to mention he's actually decent and not a douchebag."

5

I smiled in agreement. Besides basketball, Will was one of the greatest things to ever happen to me. I'd barely even talked to a boy before him. Usually guys were intimidated by me towering over them or at how much basketball dominated my life.

But not Will.

We'd been dating officially for nine months, but we'd spent at least a couple more months as friends, hanging out with our group of friends. He patiently took his time and got to know me. It wasn't just about me being shy and inexperienced—it was more about the two of us fearing Coach T's wrath.

And when he finally found out, he was furious. It wasn't just because it was *his* son I was dating. He didn't like any of his girls in serious relationships. Our head should be on the game, not on our boyfriends. Plus, there was also the fear of losing a player to pregnancy as he had a couple of years back. But finally Coach T had gotten used to the idea that Will and I were a definite couple, and that no one, not even him, could come between us.

Knowing that Will was expecting me to watch his game, I turned off the shower and then wrapped a towel around me. After blow drying my hair, I started combing through it in long strokes. "So what are you and JT doing after the game?"

Lauren waggled her auburn eyebrows. "The lake."

I rolled my eyes. "Isn't it a little cold for the lake?"

"Oh, no, we keep each other hot."

"You're terrible," I replied, packing up my bag.

"And you and Big Willy?" she asked as she brushed her strawberry blonde hair.

"Dinner and then maybe a movie back at my house."

Lauren fluttered her eyelashes. "Ah, so sweet. Do you think you'll have a milkshake at the diner, or maybe hold hands over the popcorn?"

I smacked her arm playfully. "Just because I'm having a G-rated evening compared to your R-rated one doesn't mean it's bad!"

As I started out of the locker room, Lauren nudged me. Jordan Solano stood before us in a cleavage baring top and low rise jeans. Her glossy pink lips curled into a wide smile as she talked to Coach T. "Dude, could she be more obvious?" Lauren muttered.

We started past them, and I met Coach T's eye. Over the top of Jordan's head, he winked at me. Once again, I couldn't keep from blushing. Somewhere in the last few months between basketball and Will, Coach T had become a lot more attentive towards me—enough to cause some of the other girls to be jealous. It was more than mortifying to me, and even though I wanted to say something to him about how uncomfortable it made me, I couldn't.

Lauren pushed me forward and out of my thoughts. "Why the hell does she waste her time and energy flirting with him?" she asked as we waded through the crowd.

"I don't know. I mean, Coach T isn't bad looking."

Lauren snorted. "Bad looking? Jeez, Melanie, the man could've been Brad Pitt back in his day. You think Will got his looks just from his mom?"

I shook my head.

"Plus, it doesn't hurt that he's still relatively young…he can't be forty," Lauren said.

"Thirty-eight. He was still playing college ball when Will was born," I answered.

"Right."

7

"So if he's young and good-looking, what's your point?" I asked.

Lauren scrunched her face up. "It's just he's a ball-busting asshole most of the time. And that's to us. He has no tolerance for prima donnas like Jordan."

"Yeah, but that's just on the court and in practice. He's different in the classroom. I mean, Coach T is everybody's favorite teacher."

"True. But dude, who wants to crush and flirt with a teacher? Ew."

I bobbed my head enthusiastically in agreement. Loaded down with our athletic bags, Lauren and I made our way up into the bleachers. We climbed into the packed student section a little into the first quarter.

The guys' game was tight. Will took his dad's comments to heart because he played harder than I'd seen him in a long time. Several times during the game, I'd glance over at Coach T and his wife who were sitting a couple of rows up from us. By his beaming look of pride, I could tell Coach T was enjoying Will's performance as well.

The buzzer rang, signaling the end to another Newton High victory. Will received the same treatment by his teammates as I had. He grinned at me and pumped his fist as they swept him off the court in a wave of excitement.

We stood around talking to a few people before Lauren's boyfriend, JT, motioned to her from down on the court.

She grinned. "Guess I'm being summoned by Mr. 'Why should I take a shower when I'm just gonna get all sweaty again in a few minutes?'"

I laughed. "Whatever. I'll talk to you tomorrow then."

"Mkay!" she called over her shoulder. She hustled down the steps to jump into JT's arms. He smacked her on the butt before they headed to the door. I eased back down on the bleacher and started sorting through my texts.

It wasn't long before someone tapped me on the shoulder, and I whirled around.

It was Will.

"Hey beautiful," he said, with a grin.

"You're not showering?" I asked.

"Nope, I just wanna be with you."

"Okay," I replied as I began to gather up my athletic bag and purse.

"Do you mind me all stinky and sweaty?"

I grinned. "Of course not."

Will grabbed my bag and threw it over his other shoulder. "Um, that's awfully chivalrous of you, but I think I can manage," I mused.

"Whatever, whatever."

As we headed out into the parking lot, I turned to Will. "So where are we going to eat?"

"Anywhere you want to." Then with a sheepish grin, he said, "Uh, well, anywhere that's cheap. I haven't been getting in any work hours with practice and all."

"McDonalds sound good?"

"Awesome."

After we pulled into the McDonalds down the road from the school, Will asked, "Are you sure you don't mind eating here?"

"Of course I don't. Maybe you could think about letting me pay every once in awhile?"

He shook his head. "Oh no, I don't think so. It's one thing to let you carry your own bags, but pay for dinner? Nope, not happening."

"Okay, suit yourself."

"That's probably the only thing my dad ever lectured me on that I actually agreed with."

I laughed. "Words of wisdom by Coach T?"

Will snorted. "Unfortunately yes."

He held the door open for me, and then we got in line. After we'd ordered dinner for a little over ten dollars, we headed to a table.

I'd barely opened my nuggets by the time Will had scarfed down his quarter pounder. "Um, hungry much?"

"I'm always starved after a game," he mumbled through a mouthful of fries.

"Want some of my nuggets?"

"If you're sure you don't want them..."

I slid the container over to him. "I just wish I could eat like you and never gain weight."

"Aw, baby, you always look good to me," he drawled.

"Yeah, yeah. My only saving grace is your dad runs my ass off at practice."

"Seriously, sometimes I don't know how you guys stand playing for him." Will shuddered dramatically. "What an egomaniac!"

I twirled the straw in my chocolate milkshake. I was used to these comments from Will about Coach T. As an only child, Will was supposed to have the best grades, the best after-school activities, and be an all-star athlete.

"He's really not that bad," I protested.

Will smiled. "You're just saying that because you're his little star!"

"I am not."

"Oh yes, you are. 'Melanie has the best hook shot', and 'Melanie plays defense like there's no tomorrow'," he said, mimicking Coach T.

"Whatever," I said, shaking my head.

"You're his shining star, babe, whether or not you like to admit it." Will waggled his eyebrows. "Sometimes I think he's got a serious jonsing for you."

"Ew!" I cried, throwing my wadded up napkin at him. "That's not funny."

Will winked at me. "What you don't think he's crushing on you?"

A chill went over me, and I shivered. "No, I don't. He doesn't think of me that way at all! I'm his team captain. And most importantly, I'm his *son's* girlfriend."

"Yeah, well, you're the one getting on the praise while I have to hear what a worthless tool I am half of the time," he grumbled.

I reached over and took his hand in mine. "I'm sorry."

His hardened face quickly turned into a smile. "Hey, don't be sorry."

"Okay," I said, with a yawn.

Will raised his eyebrows. "Man, am I that boring?"

I ducked my head. "No, I'm just tired, that's all."

He squeezed my hand. "I was just teasing you, Mel." When I glanced up, I met his amused gaze. "Come on, let's go."

"But I'm not ready to go home."

"Oh really?"

"No, I wanna stay with you."

His eyes crinkled with pleasure at my response. "I guess we could go back to your house and watch some movies."

"Something romantic?" I asked, giving him my best pleading look.

Will sighed and then raised his gaze to the ceiling. "Lord, please deliver me from the sappiness I'm about to see."

I smacked his arm playfully. "You know you secretly like them."

He snorted as he started gathering up our trash. "I swear, watching them has turned me into a total pansy."

"Oh, please, you're anything but a pansy," I said, as I reached over and planted a kiss on his lips.

"Hmm, and you certainly don't make me feel like a pansy!"

"Whatever," I replied with a smile.

* * *

We breezed in the back door of my house to find my parents sitting at the kitchen table. A rainbow-colored array of papers and forms were scattered around them. "Oh jeez, looks like someone's getting an early jump on tax time," Will said.

"Every year, Dad swears they're going to do their own taxes, and then every year Mom just takes everything to the accountant," I said under my breath.

Will suppressed a laugh by coughing into his hand.

"Hey guys," I called.

Dad took off his glasses. "Hey there. Boy, were those some nail biters tonight," he commented.

"Thanks."

"Want something to drink?" I asked Will.

"Sure. Got any popcorn?"

I laughed. "Let me fix us some."

"I'll get it," Mom offered, heading into the pantry. I grabbed a few sodas out of the refrigerator while she put the popcorn in. As I watched the bag rise and expand in the microwave, Will and my dad ran through the games like ESPN announcers.

The moment the microwave dinged, I cleared my throat. "Okay, okay, enough with the play by play. Will and I are going to watch a movie."

My dad chuckled. "Oh dear, poor Will. The glory of victory…and the agony of defeat!"

Will snorted. "You got that right, Mr. Reeves."

"Hey, whose side are you on?" I asked.

Dad smiled. "I just know you and your sweet, sappy romance movies…you're too much like your mother."

"Yeah, yeah," I mumbled, but I smiled in spite of myself. Will and I took the drinks and popcorn in the living room and then settled in on the couch. "And what are we watching?" Will asked, after swigging down half of his coke.

"*Sense and Sensibility*."

As I flicked on the TV, he forced a smile. "Peachy."

I leaned over and brought my lips to his. By the time the credits finished rolling, our tongues were waging war against each other. Will's hand had just begun roaming over my body when I suddenly pulled away. "Movie is on," I panted.

He groaned. "Are you serious?"

I jerked my head to the kitchen. "Besides, Mom and Dad are in the next room."

Holding my breath, I waited for his response. Any other guy would have sulked or demanded we go

13

somewhere to finish what we started. Any other guy would have dumped me months ago because I hadn't gone all the way with him.

But not Will.

The mention of my parents was the douse of cold water he needed. He straightened up and then downed the rest of his coke. He grabbed the popcorn off the table and pulled me to him. I rested my head against his chest. "This is my favorite position," I murmured.

"Yeah, I could talk to you about positions," he retorted through a mouthful of popcorn.

I elbowed him. "Watch it."

He grinned. "Okay, okay, *why* is it your favorite position?"

I stared up at him and smiled. "Because if I lean my ear in, I can hear your heart beating."

The muscles in his jaw tensed. "Melanie…"

I rolled my eyes. "I know. Stop being such a sentimental sap."

He shook his head. "No, that's not it."

"Then what is it?"

"I've been thinking about next year."

I frowned. "Will, please. I don't want to talk about that—"

"Would you let me finish?"

"Okay."

"I've decided not to go to Duke."

I popped out of my seat like a jack-in-the-box. "What do you mean? It's always been yours and your dad's dream to go there."

Shrugging, Will replied, "Well, things change. Dreams change….people change."

"But I don't understand."

Will broke a piece of popcorn apart between his fingers. "It's just I like what you and I have. I like it so much that I don't want to jeopardize it by going far away from you."

My heart fluttered in my chest. "Are you serious?"

He nodded. "Yeah, I am."

Slowly, a smile crept on my face. "You're really going to stay closer to home because of me?"

"Yep."

I threw my arms around him and kissed him. "That's wonderful, Will."

"I thought you'd like it."

I shook my head. "But I can't let you do that."

"Why not?"

"For starters, what about your scholarship?"

"It just so happens that I got an offer from Georgia Tech with the same deal."

I squealed. "I can't believe it! When were you planning on telling me?"

"I just decided this afternoon."

Happiness bubbled over in me. I didn't think; I just acted by reaching over, throwing my arms around his neck, and kissing him.

"Hey, you better watch it," he murmured, against my lips.

I pulled away to stare into his eyes. "Oh, I'm sorry. It's just…You don't know what this means to me—us not having to be separated." I bit my lip before saying, "I love you so much."

"I love you, too." Cocking an eyebrow, a wicked grin slunk across Will's face. "You know, you could walk me out to the car and show me a little bit how much you love me."

I laughed. "Do you ever stop being a horndog?"

15

"Nope."

I sighed. "All right, I'll give you a little victory gift before you leave." His grin widened at the prospect of some third base action, but I shook my head. "First, you gotta watch the movie."

He growled against my neck. "Why do I gotta pay to play?"

My hand slid down his chest to rest at the waist of his pants. "Because those are the rules of *my* game."

"It's time we rewrote the rules," he said.

"Maybe it is," I said, tentatively.

Will's head jerked away from my collarbone, and he stared into my eyes. "Whoa, whoa. Really?"

"Yeah," I murmured. I felt the intensity of his stare on me, and I realized I needed to give him an answer. "I know you've been so patient with me, Will. I've always wanted to wait not only until I was in love with someone and they loved me back, but until I knew I had a future with them." I didn't tell Will that witnessing the mistakes that my older sister, Natalie, had gotten into by sleeping around made me especially cautious. I stared into Will's eyes and smiled. "I think I'm ready now."

He exhaled noisily. "Wow, that's an interesting turn of events!"

I gave him a shy smile. "February break is coming up in a few weeks. We could go somewhere— somewhere nice."

He didn't say anything for a minute. My heart seemed to slow to a crawl waiting his response. Then he grinned.

And I knew things couldn't get much better.

Chapter Two: *Jordan*

I stared at the Budweiser clock hanging over the bar. Inside its worn hands lay the last shreds of my sanity. When the big hand finally, miraculously, inched over seven, I squealed with joy. I untied the apron from my waist and flung it under the counter. "It's quitting time for me, losers."

Marcus and Anthony laughed while my boss, Manny, glared at me. "Whatever. You just behave yourself tonight, and you sure as hell better be on time and not hung-over tomorrow!"

I spun on my heels and blew Manny a kiss. "Night Boss Man."

"Smart ass," he muttered under his breath.

I'd barely gotten out the door when a horn honked in the parking lot. My best friend, Tara, sat behind the wheel of a silver Mercedes bought with her Daddy's guilt money while our other friend, Brandi, had claimed shotgun privileges.

"Hey bitches!" I exclaimed as I threw my stuff in the back.

"Hi slut. How were the sausages tonight?" Brandi asked with a grin.

I snorted. "Don't ask." Fiorenza's might have been the best Italian restaurant in town, but they seemed to hire only perverted waiters who loved staring at my ass. "Gah working is such a drag. Not to mention, I'm never gonna get this linguini smell out without a shower."

17

"Why don't you drown yourself in body spray and see if it helps?" Tara suggested.

"I seriously doubt it," I grumbled.

I tore off my work shirt and tossed on the floorboard. The icy winter air stung my chest as I dug in my bag for my clean shirt. The car next to us began honking. I glanced over to see a carload of sophomore boys. Hanging out of the windows, they whistled and gestured towards me. "Yeah, baby! Take it off! Wanna party tonight?"

Without a second thought, I raised my hand up and flipped them off. They roared with laughter and then peeled off when the light turned green.

"Dickheads."

I pulled the shirt over my head and stretched it over last year's Christmas present from my mom—my Double D implants. I nodded in satisfaction as the shirt fit me like a second skin. I caught Tara's reflection in the mirror. "I'm *so* jealous. My parents said I couldn't have implants until graduation."

I snorted. "Yeah, well, if your mom was as flat as my mom used to be, she would probably give in quicker."

"So who are you scamming on tonight?" Brandi asked.

"No one in particular. You?"

When Brandi didn't respond, Tara sighed. "Give it up, Brandi. *He* has a girlfriend."

I slid my Nikes off and glanced at the front seat. "Who has a girlfriend?"

Brandi pinched her lips together and stared out the window. "Hello?" I asked again as I unbuttoned my pants.

"Will Thompson," Tara replied for Brandi.

18

I groaned. "Come on, not Thompson. He and Golden Goddess have been dating forever."

"I hear she's still a virgin," Brandi countered, as if that one technicality meant Will was a stud in play.

Crumpling my khakis into the bag, I began wiggling my jeans over my hips. "It doesn't matter if she's a virgin or not. He's crazy about her, and she's obviously doing some kinda of action to keep him interested. Give it up and move on. There's got to be somebody else there you'd like to date."

"At least I wanna date high school guys," she muttered under her breath.

I flung my head up, tossing my dark hair out of my face. "What did you say?"

Tara glanced from me to Brandi. Her expression silently pleaded for a change in the conversation. Brandi ignored her and turned in her seat to glare at me. "Don't act all innocent, Jordan. I know you've got the hots for Coach T."

I stiffened at the sound of his name. He was the unmentionable—the thoughts I acknowledged only to myself and once in a drunken sob story to Tara. By her wide eyes in the rear view mirror, I knew she hadn't blabbed to Brandi.

I flicked my hair. "So what if I think he's hot?"

Brandi shook his head. "He's a married man, *and* he's a teacher!"

"So?"

Her eyes widened. "All you can say is *so*?"

"We're seniors. I'm eighteen, and we'll be graduating in five months. It's not a big deal."

"But he's married."

"That doesn't mean he's happy, or that he isn't looking for someone to make him happy," I retorted.

I'd heard that line a million times from my mother. Most of the time, she was screaming it into the phone at a wife of one of the married men she slept with.

Snapping open my compact, I shot Brandi a look. "When you slept with your dad's business partner over New Years, did I say anything?"

A strangled gasp escaped her lips. "I told you I was drunk!"

"Yeah, you told me that. *But*," I emphasized, "how am I to know it's the truth?"

When Brandi didn't say anything, I smacked my lips, which shimmered with newly applied gloss. "So why don't you mind your own business, and I'll mind mine?"

She flounced back in her seat and crossed her arms over her chest. "Whatever."

Thankfully, we then pulled up at the school. "Nothing like making an entrance," Tara giggled.

I peered at the clock. "Yeah, I guess the Varsity girls' game is almost over." At the mention of the *girls'* game, my body tingled. *He* wouldn't notice me as long as he coached. But as soon as the buzzer sounded, he'd be free.

We opened the doors, and silence echoed throughout the gym. I craned my neck to see Golden Goddess, aka Melanie Reeves, at the foul line. A quick peek at the scoreboard showed we were down by one point. If Miss Thing could make her two shots, then we'd win.

I'd known Melanie the last four years of high school. We weren't exactly what you'd call "friends". She had her A-Crowd Group while my friends and I were out on the fringes of the popular set. How she ever got Will Thompson I'll never know. Brandi was

20

warranted a good crush on him since he was a babe. But he was too goody-two shoes for me, just like Miss Thing.

My gaze flicked over to Coach T or Mark Thompson or *my* Mark. He knelt at the edge of the court, one hand over his heart. He flinched as the first shot banged against the rim before finally going in. "YES!" he shouted, pumping his fist and grinning at Melanie.

Motionless, I stood analyzing his every move. I tried to imagine what it would be like to be Melanie right now. To have that kind of pressure bearing down on you—it made me shudder. The crowd quieted down as Melanie bounced the ball twice before she aimed. It soared through the air and crisply swooshed through the net.

The crowd rose to their feet, and Coach T rushed the court. As he gathered Melanie into his arms and rained praise down on her, I'd never wanted to be someone else so much, especially not Melanie Reeves, the goody two-shoes everyone adored. A tingle rang through me as I remembered what those arms and hands felt like. Course, Miss Thing had never felt them quite like I had.

If you'd told me six months ago I'd be having an affair with a married teacher, especially Coach T, I would have said you were screwed up in the head. But that was before I was sentenced to a month of Saturday School detention torture with Coach T as the teacher. Yeah, nothing blows like school from eight to noon on one of your days off.

When no one showed up for the second session, Coach T and I spent four hours alone in the In School Suspension room. Instead of making me work on missing assignments, we just talked and laughed. The next Saturday, we passed notes while the others worked. And then after my last detention, he came to eat at Fiorenza's. We had our first make-out session that day in one of the storage rooms. And then it wasn't too long before we were sleeping together.

Tara nudged me. "Dude, Jo, you are so out of it tonight!"

"Sorry," I mumbled.

"I must've called your name like five times." She pulled me along after I saw Coach T head for the locker-room. We bumped and jostled our way through the crowd. When someone touched my ass, I whirled around.

Andy Poletti grinned down at me. "Hey Jordan, looking good."

"Touch my ass again, and I'll kick you in the balls!" I growled.

"Ooh, that's sounds hot."

I rolled my eyes and started to walk off. "Come on. When are you gonna go out with me again?" he asked.

"Never."

"But we had such a good time," he replied, with a wink.

"Ugh, I'd hardly call ten minutes in the back of your car a good time."

"You seemed to enjoy it then."

"Fuck off, Andy."

I stalked away and caught up with Tara. She threw me a questioning glance. "Don't ask," I snapped.

By the time we found a seat in the sea of people, the boys' team was about to take the court. "Will you watch my purse for a second?" I asked.

"Where are you going?" Tara asked.

"I'll be back," I called over my shoulder. I headed the opposite way down the stairs to the girl's locker-room. Coach T stood outside the door, reading his stat book with his assistant coach.

"Hey," I said, with a grin.

"Hey yourself," he replied.

"Great game."

"Yeah, Mel really pulled through for us, didn't she?"

I nodded. "Those last two shots were tight."

Coach T handed the stat book to Coach Rossen. "Thanks Dave. You can take this with you."

"Sure. See you Monday."

As soon as Coach Rossen walked off, Coach T's demeanor changed. He gave me a wink before his eyes roamed over my body. "That was total bullshit you know."

"What?"

He grinned. "Saying you enjoyed the game. I'll bet ten bucks you didn't get here until the very end."

I laughed. "Well, you know me too well, don't you?"

He glanced around before he responded. "I've missed you," he replied in a hoarse whisper.

My heart fluttered, and I wanted to gasp, *"You have?"*, but instead, I kept my cool. "Then you've been a naughty boy thinking about me."

He leaned closer to me. "I can't wait until Monday to be with you."

I curled my lips into a seductive smile. "So what are you going to do about it?"

His eyebrows shot up. "Now?"

"Why not?"

"Will is about to take the court."

"You want me so bad then prove it to me," I countered.

At that moment, Melanie and her basketball BFF Lauren Elrod, came out of the locker-room. I quickly changed gears.

"So are you really gonna dock me a whole letter grade for not dressing out? That's so unfair. You're supposed to be everyone's favorite coach," I whined for their benefit.

I shuddered with jealousy as Coach T grinned and winked at Melanie. When they were gone, he inched closer to me. "Meet me outside behind the old concession stand in five minutes."

"All right."

I waved bye to him and walked away. I backtracked around the court and went out the front doors. I glanced around. No one was paying any attention. It was dark as hell outside, and I could barely see in front of me. Stumbling, I made my way across campus to the run down area where the old football field had been.

When I turned the corner of the concession stand, Coach T grabbed me. I melted into him as his lips crushed against mine. I couldn't see anything in the dark, but I didn't need too. All I needed was the feel of his hands on me.

And I knew that was a certainty.

Cold air stung my bare stomach as he jerked my shirt out of my jeans. I sucked in a rasping breath before he replaced the iciness with his warm palms. They slid up my ribcage to cup my breasts, kneading them roughly. I shivered with excitement as our tongues battled each other. Keeping one hand on my breast, he brought the other down to undo my jeans almost effortlessly. He thrust his hand inside to delve into my panties, seeking out my warmth.

"Jordan, I want you so much," he breathed into my ear.

As his eager fingers slid inside me, I panted, "Can't you see how much I want you?"

"Hmm, baby, you're always so hot and wet for me. I could stay buried inside you all the time."

Those words were all the encouragement I needed. My fingers tugged at the button on his pants. Once I had the zipper down, I shoved his underwear and pants down over his hips.

When he rammed me back against the metal wall of the concession stand, I cried out. The cold pierced my naked skin like a thousand knives.

His fingers stopped working their magic inside me. "What's wrong?"

Now my teeth were chattering. "The w-wall is c-cold."

"I know how to fix that," he murmured, as he withdrew from me to dig a condom out of his wallet.

After he slid it on, he grabbed my bare ass and lifted me to wrap my legs around his waist. In one harsh thrust, he buried himself inside me, pounding me back against the icy wall. But I didn't feel the cold. True to his word, Coach T fixed everything. His thrusts were rushed and frantic as I grinded myself against him.

All too quickly it was over, and I wanted to cry. The fact that I needed to be connected to him so much scared me. The one thing I wouldn't admit to my friends, my mom, or anyone else was I was in love. I hated to admit it even to myself. Somewhere between the flirtation and the affair, I'd fallen for him. He was everything I could ever imagine wanting.

After he zipped up his pants, he kissed me one last time. "Monday as usual?"

"Yes," I replied, breathlessly.

"Good."

He peered around the side of the concession stand and then started jogging back across campus. I waited a good ten minutes before I started back to the gym. I skidded to a stop when I saw Tara standing outside the door. "Where were you?"

"Oh, Andy wanted to talk to me for a minute."

She eyed me suspiciously, but she didn't say anything. "Come on. The guy's game is already in the second quarter."

I smoothed my shirt and hair one last time and then followed her inside. My stomach churned when I saw Coach T with his wife. She sat on the bleacher above him, draping her arms over his neck. I argued against the nagging feeling in the pit of my stomach. After all, it was *her* hanging all over him, not the other way around. He didn't really want her anymore—he just wanted me.

I turned my head and tried to focus on the game, but all I could do was think about him. When I kept grinning like an idiot about our quickie, Tara rolled her eyes.

"Did you go out to the parking lot and hook-up with Andy?"

"Ew, no! Why would you think that?"

"Cause you're acting all sex glowy."

I snorted. "I promise if I touched Andy, it would be to slap the shit out of him."

Brandi was talking up some guy beside her, so Tara leaned over to me. "I saw you talking to Coach T."

I stared straight ahead, not allowing my face to betray anything I was feeling. "Yeah, I ran into him on the way to the bathroom."

"You didn't go to the bathroom," she argued softly.

"Why don't you say what you want to or forget it?" I asked. My knuckles were white from twisting my purse strap over and over in my hands.

Tara hesitated, biting her lip. "Is there really something going on between you and Coach T?"

My heartbeat accelerated in my chest. "Jesus, no! Can't I think a man is hot without it meaning something else?"

She shrugged. "You just seem really flirty with him."

"I flirt with everyone," I argued.

"I know," she said. "But there's something about the way you look at him. It's different."

"It's *nothing*," I emphasized.

Tara nodded, but I could tell she didn't completely believe me. For the rest of the night, I tried to reign in my behavior so I wouldn't make anyone else suspicious.

Chapter Three: *Melanie*

Squeak, squeak, squeak, swoosh, swoosh, swoosh.
It was Monday afternoon, and my ears hummed with
the familiar sounds of Coach's T's kill and drill
practice sessions. As captain and guard, I ran play
after play, bringing the ball down the court safely until
it passed to the next player's hands. But I didn't feel
truly successful at my job unless the ball also made its
way into the net.

The sound of Coach T's whistle caused me to
screech to a halt. "Becca, go in for Melanie," he
ordered. Becca raced off the bench without a question.
"Mel!" He waved me over. I handed the ball to her
before trotting off the court. "Yeah, Coach."

He motioned towards the players. "I want you to
tell me what's going on with the Packed Ten play.
Nothing seems to be working right."

I nodded.

"All right, let's run a Packed Ten," he barked. The
rest of the girls ran the play at least three times before
Coach T turned to me and arched his eyebrow.
"Whatcha think?"

I closed my eyes and saw the play again in my
mind. Although I hated to admit it, I knew it was
Lauren's fault. She kept forgetting to stay with her
man. I bit my lip. With my eyes still closed, Coach T's
voice hummed close to my ear. "I guess you agree
with what I'm thinking."

My blue eyes snapped open to meet his dark ones.
Amusement twinkled in them. "You've got too much

honor, Mel. You'll never make it as a head coach if you can't learn that."

"Who says I want to coach someday?" I asked, even though I knew the answer. There was no doubt I wanted to become a teacher and coach just like him. I'd realized that freshman year when I sat at half court and listened to one of his pep talks. He made rules, technique, and skills so clear, and he made the game like nothing I'd ever experienced before. I wanted to bring that same enthusiasm to girls someday. To have them change their view that basketball was just a sport and to embrace it as something so much more than they ever imagined.

Reaching over he poked the place above my heart. "That right there. It tells me you're gonna make a hell of a teacher and coach someday. If," he paused and grinned, "you learn that in basketball, you have to be tough with your emotions. There's no friends, no loyalty—just the game."

I smiled. "All right. Lauren's screwing up the play. You want me to tell her that and then make her run until she gets her act together?"

Coach T cocked his eyebrows at me. "Ah, look whose showing her tough side." He looked from me out to the court. "I tell you what, Terminator. I'll let you off the hook this time. I'll call Lauren over and chew her out. How's that?"

Inwardly, I cringed. Lauren had a temper, and I dreaded having to go into the locker room with her after one of Coach T's 'Come to Jesus' bawl outs he was famous, or maybe infamous, for.

He nudged me playfully. "You don't look too convinced, Mel."

"No, no, you're right. Go ahead and call her out."

Coach T grinned at me before blowing his whistle. Becca came back to warm the bench some more, I jogged back onto the court, and Lauren got blessed out on the sidelines.

At the end of practice, Coach T spared me from the wrath of Lauren by saying, "Mel, run these balls into the athletic closet for me, and then bring me one of the pumps."

I nodded and hustled off the court. The smell of age and rubber greeted me as I opened the closet door. Grunting, I pulled the rack of balls inside before going in search of one of the pumps. The closet needed a serious spring cleaning.

My shoes got caught in an old basketball net, causing me to pitch forward. "Fabulous, let me kill myself all over a stupid pump," I grumbled. I scanned the rickety shelves. "All right, Coach T. Where the hell did you put the pump?" Finally, I found it on a top shelf. As I pulled it off, the shelf made an odd creaking noise, and then everything went black.

And after that moment, it would take a long time to come out of the darkness that enveloped me

Chapter Four: *Melanie*

With my head pounding, I shakily reached for the door handle of my car. My hands trembled so hard I could barely get the key into the ignition. As soon as the car sputtered to life, I brought my foot down hard on the accelerator and pealed out of the parking lot. All I wanted was to get home.

As hard as it was, I tried keeping my mind on the drive. Along the familiar streets to my house, I counted mailboxes and the painted lines on the road— anything to not think. As long as I didn't think, I couldn't remember…and as I long as I couldn't remember, it hadn't happened.

I hoped for a quick escape to my bedroom when I got home, but I wasn't so lucky. The moment I dragged myself through the garage door, my mother pounced on me. "Sweetie, are you okay?"

"It's just a bump, Mom," I argued, through my pain filled haze. I stared past her—just a couple of steps, and I could make it up the back staircase. Just a couple of stairs and I could be to my room.

Mom felt along my hairline. "I don't know, Melanie. We may need to get it examined."

"No, I'm not going to the hospital!"

Mom stared at me in surprise at my outburst. I forced a smile to my lips. "It's fine. Coach Murray looked me over. Don't you think if it were something serious he would've called an ambulance?" I grabbed a glass out of the cabinet before fumbling in the medicine drawer for Advil. Then it hit me. "Wait, how did you know about my head?"

"Coach T called a few minutes ago to make sure you were all right."

The glass slid out of my hands and crashed onto the floor. My face flushed with embarrassment. "Whoops," I said, sheepishly as I eyed the broken glass.

"Here, sweetie. Take the Advil to the table and have a seat. I'll get you some water."

"Okay," I said. I gingerly stepped over the glass and then made my way to a chair. Without thinking, I plopped down on the hard oak. Pain shot through my lower abdomen with such intensity I bit my lip to keep from crying out. It felt like every bone in my body had been beaten, and there was a gnawing feeling in the pit of my abdomen.

"He kept apologizing over and over for letting you drive home. He said you wouldn't let him drive you. I told him it was all right." Mom set the glass down on the table and smiled at me. "After all, Daddy and I know how stubborn you can be."

I opened my mouth to protest when a knock came at the back door. My stomach clenched into knots. *Please don't let it be him…Please…I'll start screaming if it is.*

"Wonder who that could be?" Mom asked.

When she flung open the door, my heart stopped and restarted.

It was Will.

He barely acknowledged Mom. Instead, his eyes frantically searched the kitchen. The minute he saw me, he crossed the room in two long strides. He knelt down beside me, taking my hands into his. "Are you okay?"

With my cheeks burning, I ducked my head and whispered, "I'm fine."

Will wrapped his arms around me. Even though his breath was hot on my neck, I shivered. "Dad said you got a pretty bad bump on the head, and you were out cold for a few minutes."

"It wasn't that long," I muttered.

He pulled away to stare into my eyes. There was such a mixture of love and concern that my heart ached. His fingers cupped my chin, pulling my face to his. When his lips met mine, I shuddered and jerked away.

Will smiled, and then whispered, "My bad. I know how you feel about me kissing you in front of your mom."

I just stared down at my hands. Mom walked over to us. "It's awfully sweet of you to come over and check on Melly."

"The moment Dad called me, I just ran out the door. He must've thought I was crazy racing over here for a bump that didn't need an ambulance or anything. I guess I could've called, but I knew I wouldn't feel right until I saw for myself she was okay."

Mom brought her hand to heart and gushed, "Oh, that's so thoughtful of you!"

Will's grinned widened. "Ah, I'm even more of a knight in shining armor." He looked at me. "Guess who has a *major* English paper due tomorrow?"

"Oh, no," I moaned, bringing my hand to my forehead.

"Oh, *yes*, we do. So, I thought you might need some help."

"I completely forgot. Ugh, how am I going to get through an essay with my head throbbing?"

"Because I'm going to help you," Will replied.

"Help me write it, or help me cheat by using yours?" I asked.

Will laughed. "A little of both."

I bit my lip. "Look, I really don't think this is a good time. I mean, I'll be a day or two late with it, and Ms. Anderson can just take ten points off."

Will reached out to cup my face. "Just let me help you, okay?"

I didn't have the strength to argue anymore, so I merely nodded. "But I really need to shower first," I whispered.

"I told you I liked you all sweaty," Will said, with a wink.

I closed my eyes and nodded my head. "I know."

His thumb rubbed against my cheek. "All right, beautiful. Take your shower, and I'll just fire up the laptop while I wait."

When we both started upstairs, Mom opened her mouth to protest, but then snapped it shut. I knew she didn't like the idea of me showering with Will up there. I sighed in exasperation. "I'll leave the bedroom door open, okay?"

She nodded and smiled. "Okay."

Twice I faltered on the steps, but luckily Will was there to catch me. As we started into the bedroom, he asked, "You sure you ought to be showering?"

"I'll be fine."

"Not that I wouldn't mind rushing in there to save you!"

I glanced back at him, and he shot me a wicked grin. It caused something to turn over in me like a switch. "God, don't you ever stop thinking about sex!" I snapped.

Will arched his eyebrows. "Ouch! That bump brought out the bitchiness in you tonight. I'm seriously feeling the claws!"

I didn't say anything.

"Hmm, maybe I should leave and let you work out the essay the best way you can."

"Do whatever you want," I grumbled, as I took out a clean shirt and sweatpants from my drawer. But when I peeked at him through the shroud of hair covering my face, I saw him shake his head before sitting down at the desk.

Will began tinkering with the computer as I gathered up my things and went inside the bathroom. I didn't bother looking in the mirror. After all, I would've had to fight the urge to scream at my appearance. And I wasn't just being dramatic.

No, there was so much more.

Slowly, I peeled my clothes off. And then one stolen glance at the inside of my practice shorts sent me over the edge. I tried reasoning that it wasn't just the shorts. I mean, I'd been teetering on the brink for an hour now. It might have been the sheer force of trying to keep my sanity in check—to block what had happened out of my mind—or to swear on my life that I would never admit it had happened.

But deep down I knew it was the shorts that sent me truly over the edge. The ones marked blood red with evidence of what had transpired on the futon in Coach T's office.

I snatched the towel off the rack and buried my face in it. Muffled sobs reverberated against the terry cloth fabric. Defeated, I slunk into the shower. With the water pounding in the stall, my screams and sobs were drowned out. I slid down the side of shower tile, letting the water scald me. Even as splotches of red blotted my skin, I never turned away. It soothed something deeply troubled within me.

Biting into the towel, I choked off my cries. I fought to find anything or anyone else to blame for what happened. I cursed the stupid rack because it had messed up my entire night. Without it, I would have never been left alone in the gym with him. He would have never had the opportunity.

Everything I'd fought to suppress in the last hour came flashing back into my mind—as electric and dangerous as the heat storms we had in the summer. Suddenly, I was no longer in my bathroom.

I was in Coach T's office.

My head throbbed, and I reclined on the futon in the corner. A long eternity seemed to have stretched by since Coach T had ushered all my teammates out the door. They'd been hanging around to make sure I was okay. He reassured them I was fine, and they should get on home.

Something cold pressed against my forehead and caused me to jump. When my eyes met Coach T's, he laughed. "Easy Mel, it's just an ice pack."

"Oh, thanks." I took it from him.

"That was quite a bump on the head," he said, as he sat down beside me.

"Must've been. I don't even remember coming to your office."

"You didn't. After you got hit by the shelf and pump, I found you sprawled out in the floor and brought you in here."

It was then that I wanted to crawl under the futon and die of embarrassment. The thoughts of him picking me up were completely mortifying. My face flushed. "Oh God, that's right. I remember you carrying me now."

He laughed at my expression. "It's okay, Mel. It's not like you gave me a hernia or something!"

"No, it's not okay," I moaned. "It's totally humiliating!"

"Just to you it is," he replied, turning back to his desk.

"Ugh, I bet the team is going to give me crap tomorrow about being such a spaz."

"You aren't a spaz. I've been asking the Booster Club to repair that shelf for years. It could have happened to anyone."

"But it happened to me," I countered.

Spinning around in his seat, Coach T said, "We're lucky that Coach Murray was still here to check you over. I was just thankful you weren't going to need an ambulance."

It was then I remembered the burly face of Coach Murray, one of the trainers for the football team who had once been an EMT, bending over me while I was still lying on the floor of the athletic closet.

I sighed with relief. The last thing I would have wanted was the big production of the ambulance being called with all the sirens and flashing lights. That would have been a nightmare!

I leaned forward. Even though there was no window on his office door, I knew it had to be late, so I started to stand up. "I guess I better get going."

Coach T rose from his chair to place a hand on my shoulder. "I don't know about that. I think you're still too woozy to be driving."

"Um, I guess so," I murmured. Slowly, I eased back down. As he joined me on the futon, his hand lingered on me, his fingertips feathering back and forth on my bare arm.

I shifted the ice pack. When I did, I found Coach T staring at me. "W-what?" I stammered, embarrassed by the intensity of his stare. "Oh God, is my head already swelling?"

He laughed. "Nope. But it should because you're just so damn beautiful."

"No, I'm not."

He shook his head. "That's what I love about you, Mel. You're so unaware of how beautiful and alluring you are."

"You must be thinking of my sister, Natalie. *She's* the alluring one, not me."

He brought his hand to my cheek. His thumb traced a line from my cheekbone to my ear. "Trust me, Mel, I've been with a hell of a lot of women, so I know beautiful when I see it."

Heat once again rose in my cheeks at the reference to his sex life. Coach T mistook my reaction. "You don't have to blush when you're given an honest to goodness compliment. You *are* beautiful, Melanie. I mean, you were this brace-faced, awkward little mouse of a thing when you first walked in my gym four years ago. Talent out the ass, but so unsure of yourself." He laughed. "Well, maybe you still are unsure of yourself. But, four years later you've grown to be one of the most beautiful young women I've ever seen."

Coach T's flattery made me uncomfortable and caused my heart to flutter uneasily. The room closed in around me, and I felt like I wasn't getting any air. His presence loomed over me, and I didn't like his closeness—the way his leg brushed against mine or the feel of his hand on my shoulder.

It wasn't like I'd never been alone with him before. But there was something different about this time. My instincts told me something was wrong. And more than anything, I wanted to be out of there.

"Um, it's late. I better get home now," I said.

Before I could raise myself off the futon, Coach T's mouth crushed against mine. I felt the moisture of his tongue as it pushed against my lips, forcing them open. When his tongue darted into my mouth, I jerked away like I'd been stunned by a taser. I trembled and tried to get my bearings.

"Coach T, you shouldn't have done that!" I protested.

His arm snaked around me, nudging me against him. As his breath burned on my cheek, it was like there was no escaping him. "Oh, but I should have. You don't know how long I've wanted to do that. I've had my eye on you for so long, and I've waited patiently."

As the magnitude of his words crashed over me, I shuddered. No, no, no! This couldn't be happening. I had to be wrong. Coach T would never do this to me. He'd never kiss me when he shouldn't or tell me he'd had his eye on me for a long time. No, it couldn't be true. I'd been hit on the head and was hallucinating

"It isn't right!" *You shouldn't be arguing with him. You should be getting the hell out of here!* my mind reasoned.

"What's wrong with kissing a beautiful girl?"

I don't feel beautiful right now. I feel cheap and dirty. "But I-I belong to Will!" I argued, as I swatted his hand away and tried to get up, but he eased me back down.

Coach T shook his head and smiled. "You don't belong to anyone, Mel. You're your own person." His hand swept up my leg to rest on my thigh. "And I love you."

"N-No…you can't. You're married."

"So? It doesn't mean I don't love you."

"But I love Will."

He snorted. "Will's just a boy. What does he know? You deserve a man to teach you about love not some fumbling kid." I continued trying to push his hand away, as his breath hovered over my ear, "Better yet, you need *me* to teach you about love."

I stared into his eyes. My voice became a small whisper. "Please, don't say that."

"Melanie, surely you realized how much I've wanted you?"

Slowly, I shook my head.

"What about at Christmas when I kissed you under the mistletoe?"

I cringed as I thought back to that night. Will had invited me to his house when his parents were having a party. We stayed upstairs most of the night, watching movies and talking, fooling around a little. When I'd gone downstairs to get something to drink, Coach T had pinned me against the kitchen door and kissed me under the mistletoe. His reeking breath told me how drunk he was, so I'd tried to brush it off as nothing. Somehow it had stayed in the back of my mind.

"But you were drunk," I argued feebly.

"Maybe I was, but I wasn't too drunk to want you."

Like in a movie, the world crawled by in nightmarish slow motion. Coach T's weight smothered me, pressing me down on the futon. A voice began screaming inside of me as I clawed against him. "NO! No, please. Please don't do this!"

His breath scorched down my neck, hot with desire—the same desire that pushed against my thigh. "Just let me love you—let me love you like I've wanted to for so long, Melanie."

I shook my head. Like a captured fish on a hook, I flailed beneath him. Then as bits and pieces of my clothing were stripped away, I slowly stopped fighting. Fear gripped me like I had never experienced before in my life.

It stunned and paralyzed me.

In just a matter of seconds, I became a quadriplegic. Even though my brain screamed at my arms and legs to fight, the only thing I could move was my eyelids. But I clamped them shut, deluding myself that if I couldn't see what was going on, then it wasn't really happening.

Then I detached. I floated above myself, spiriting away from the pain that ripped through me. I was no longer in the room with Coach T moving frantically inside me. Faintly, I could hear the roar of the crowd in my ears, and the rubber smell of the basketball filled my nostrils. Happiness engulfed me.

I was on the court, and I was a star. I made basket after basket. Even three pointers flew gracefully through the air to swoosh almost effortlessly through the goal. Elation filled me as points for my team racked up on the red glow of the scoreboard. As I sprinted up and down the court, I never grew tired, nor did I ever grow faint of breath. Gazing into the stands, I saw my parents as they clapped, screamed out my name, and waved their pom-poms. The crowd rose to their feet and applauded me while my teammates patted my back and hugged me.

But more than the adulation of the fans, the love of my family, and the support of my team, it was Heaven.

And I was safe.

But that moment was fleeting, and I was sucked back into reality. It was over, and Coach T was pulling away from me. I still didn't open my eyes, even as the silent tears dripped off my cheeks.

The seconds ticked agonizingly by. I heard him straightening his clothes. Then he cleared his throat. "Jesus, Mel, I-I'm sorry."

My only reply was to involuntarily begin shaking. "I didn't know you were a…" he trailed off. His words pierced my heart with the double-edged sword of his actions. "I just assumed you and Will had been together." He gingerly touched my bare back, and I winced. "I would have taken it slower if I'd known that."

I choked off a sob. He wasn't even sorry that'd he… raped me—just that he'd taken my virginity. Finally, I opened my eyes. Without realizing it, I'd rolled away from him. I clutched my knees to my chest, trying to cover myself. I felt my t-shirt wadded beneath me. Left only with my sports bra on, I didn't know what had happened to my shorts and underwear.

"Mel, I am sorry."

I didn't know what he wanted me to say. So, I merely nodded. After all, speaking seemed foreign to me. I feared if I opened my mouth, the sobs that had built up inside me and lodged in my throat would come spewing out. Something deep within me thought they might never stop.

"I hope you can forgive me."

I refused to meet his gaze.

"I crossed the line. It won't ever happen again, I swear. I've got problems at home, Mel. I'm in therapy, and I'll get this sorted out. I swear," he pleaded.

I didn't want his apologies or his excuses. I just wanted out of there. I wanted to crawl under my covers and die of the pain and humiliation.

When I still didn't respond, he exhaled noisily. "You know, telling someone about this won't do any good."

My gaze snapped to his. "What?" I croaked.

"It's just a no-win situation for either of us. If you go to the authorities, I'm screwed. But so are you."

Horrified, I continued to stare at him. "How?"

"Because of Will."

And with that, Coach T silenced any thoughts I might have had of reporting him. So, I finally gave him the words he was so desperate for. "I won't tell anyone. Ever."

My traitorous words echoed off my ears as I came back to myself on the shower floor. A knock at the door caused me to jump. It was my mom. "Melanie, are you all right? You've been in there an awfully long time."

Speak, Melanie, a voice commanded within me. It should've been easy. I'd been doing it since I was barely a year old. But it seemed impossible. We'd even taught our two black Labs, Scout and Jem, to do it, so why couldn't I?

"Melanie?"

I dug my nails into my forearm until tears stung my eyes. The pain caused my voice to break through the levels of my consciousness. "I'm fine, Mom. Just a few more minutes, okay? The water feels really good on my head." The lie tumbled easily from my lips—far more easily than the truth ever would.

"Okay, but don't stay too much longer." She paused, and then I heard her laughter. "Will says you're going to turn into a shriveled prune."

At the mention of Will, bitter tears streaked down my face. Oh God, was I really not going to tell what had happened? Deep down, I knew what I should do. I'd seen enough television programs to know I should've come straight in and told my mom. I should have been carted off to the hospital where some stranger would poke and prod me with a rape kit, making me die a thousand deaths under the scratchy white sheet pulled up to my chin.

Then if I survived that degradation, I'd have to relive the experience itself over and over again as I told my story to investigators, maybe even as I testified at trial. In my mind, I could see a courtroom full of spectators, eagerly leaning forward in their seats to digest the juicy details.

No, no, no!

I couldn't bear that.

What about my parents? The mere thought made me tremble. I imagined the expressions that would appear on their faces—the horror, the agony, the guilt, maybe even the shame. What would news like this to do them? They'd always sworn to protect me no matter what. They'd feel like failures. Plus, I'd always been the least trouble out of my siblings. The one my parents could always depend on to stay out of trouble, therefore saving them face. But if I admitted this, then I would become the pitied child that all my parents' friends gossiped about. "Did you hear about Joe and Suzanne's daughter being raped? Yeah, it's torn them all apart."

I couldn't bear that.

Then once again my thoughts went to Will—the love of my life. The only guy who'd ever given me the time of day. The only guy I'd ever dated and kissed and fooled around with. The only guy I could ever imagine being with until death do us part. The guy who sat in my room right now doing an essay for me just so I wouldn't lose a measly ten points.

Not only would Will's father be carted off to jail, but Coach T would lose his job. He'd never coach or teach ever again. Even though anger burned within me for Coach T, the fact remained I was in love with his son. If I told the world my boyfriend's father raped me, our relationship would crumble. Will's seemingly perfect life would be shattered, and in some horrible and warped way, I would be the cause of it.

I couldn't bear that.

I silently lifted my eyes to the Heavens. I shook my head. I'd been a believer all my life. I'd gone to church religiously—I'd even been played Mary twice in our Christmas pageants.

But I wasn't Mary anymore. I was a defiled and perverse version of my former self, the "Old Melanie". Tentatively, I stood up in the shower. Then in some weird out-of-body experience I started bathing like nothing had happened.

While lathering my head, I felt the large knot forming under my skin. There was also a ragged cut

45

along my hairline, and when I rinsed my hair, there was blood in the water, even though I'd been as gentle as I could. And then I realized it wasn't from my head.

More blood loss…more loss of innocence…more evidence of what I'd lost on the futon. I shivered despite the scalding water.

Once again, I raised tear stained eyes to the ceiling. "How am I going to do this?" I murmured. Silence reverberated back at me. I don't know what I expected. Did I expect God to speak to me and tell me how to lie to the world?

When I got out of the shower, I didn't bother drying my hair. I threw on my Newton Lady Grizzlies Basketball t-shirt and my sweatpants. I opened the door to find Will hard at work. The sight of him bent over the laptop with papers scattered everywhere made my chest burn.

"Hey," I said softly.

He swiveled around in my rolling chair. "Hey, beautiful!"

For a brief instant, I didn't see him. All I saw was Coach T spinning around in his chair like he had earlier tonight. *Stop it, Melanie!*

I bit my lip and played with the drawstring on my pants. "Um, I'm sorry about being a bitch earlier."

Will shook his head. "Nah, it's okay. You've had a shitty night. And I was being a douchebag about sex."

A chill went through me, and I shuddered. Will came over to stand beside me. "You shouldn't be standing here with your hair wet in the middle of winter. Isn't it enough you got bonked in the head tonight? You don't need to get sick on top of that."

I shook my head. "No, I don't." I could feel the intensity of his stare on me. Finally, I brought my eyes to his.

"Are you okay?" he asked.

"Yeah, I'm fine."

He smiled and pulled me into his arms. My eyes closed as I was overwhelmed by the security of his embrace. No one made me feel like Will. He was like home...like my parents. I didn't want anything to ever come between us. It was a desperate feeling—one that caused a sob to build in my throat.

Will must have felt the emotions coursing through me because he whispered into my ear, "Babe, I'm here. You're all right, and I'm all right."

My eyelids fluttered open, and I smiled at him. "We're all right."

Will grinned. "That's right." He kissed the top of my head and glanced over at the desk. "But we're not going to be all right if we don't get your essay finished."

Reluctantly, I let my arms fall from him. He sat down and then spun back around in the chair. "Okay, so we're supposed to be looking for occult symbolism in *Macbeth*. Now I used…"

His voice trailed off as I eased down on the bed. My head still throbbed, and I didn't want to think about Macbeth. I just wanted to go to sleep….sleep would be an escape.

I grabbed the throw off the bottom of my bed and wrapped it around me. It wasn't long before its warmth and the soothing sound of Will's voice lulled me to sleep.

The next thing I knew I heard his soft laughter in my ear. "Hey, Sleeping Beauty, I finished your essay."

I drowsily opened my eyes to see Will's grinning face above me. "I'm sorry. I couldn't help it."

"Yeah, just be glad you dozed off before I realized it. Your mom freaked out thinking you might have a concussion. She was about ready to check your pupils, but I told her you weren't totally out."

"How come?"

"Cause you were kinda crazy while you slept."

My face burned. "I-I was."

Will nodded. "Yeah, from the noises you were making, it must've been some dream." He smiled down at me. "I sure hope I was in it."

I gazed up into his eyes so full of love, and I shook my head. "More like a nightmare I guess."

He kissed me gently. "I'm here for you. No one's gonna hurt you. I'll kick some boogey man's ass."

"I'm sure you would," I whispered.

"All right, it's eleven, and I'm gonna hit the road." He started for the door, but I pulled on his arm.

"Stay with me."

"What?"

"Stay with me until I go back to sleep." When he stared at me in surprise, I forced a smile to my lips. "You know, to kick the boogeyman's ass and all."

Will laughed. "Okay." He kicked off his shoes and lay down beside me. He pulled me into his arms, and I rested my head on his chest.

When I heard the gentle rhythm of his heart, I murmured, "My favorite position."

At that moment I realized I would do anything in the world to save what Will and I had. I'd promised Coach T I wouldn't tell anyone, and I decided it would be a vow I'd keep—regardless of what I had to say or do.

48

Chapter Five: *Jordan*

I drummed my French-manicured nails across the steering wheel, throwing another impatient glance at the clock. "What's taking him so long?" I hissed.

I was waiting for my usual Monday night hook-up to commence. It'd been two weeks since our behind the concession-stand quickie. For a moment, my aggravation subsided when I thought of how lately Coach T, or Mark as I should've thought of him, couldn't seem to get enough of me. Monday nights were set in stone, but lately, he'd texted me to meet up at least two more times.

Regardless of what I was doing, I dropped everything to meet him. Nothing filled the stretches of lonely days quite like those stolen hours we shared together.

But when I eyed the clock again, I twitched in frustration. Usually, as soon as everyone had cleared out of the building, Coach T would flick the outside lights twice. Then I knew the coast was clear, and I could go inside.

But he was thirty minutes late tonight, and I quickly texted a, "WTF is going on?" message. I wasn't gonna wait outside all night for him. Especially after I'd turned the car off fifteen minutes ago, and I was shivering in the late January cold. Well, I told myself I would leave, knowing full well I would wait for him forever.

49

My eyes caught sight of a figure in the parking lot. I squinted and recognized Melanie Reeves. Even though it was after practice, she looked like hell. Her mascara smudged across her cheeks, and her lipstick looked smeared. Geez, she could have at least taken the time to clean up before heading home.

Her car had barely left the parking lot when I saw the flick of the lights. I checked my reflection in the mirror one more time before opening the car door. My heels clicked across the pavement as I made my way to the door. The only nice thing about meeting in the practice gym was the fact there were no cameras and no fear of discovery. It was the one area of the school that had yet to be remodeled or brought into the technological age.

I found Coach T sitting at his desk, his head in his hands.

"Hey," I said softly. I reached over to run my fingers through his dark hair. He surprised me by jerking away. "What's wrong?"

He still refused to look at me. "We can't do this."

"Aren't you in the mood tonight?"

He raised his head to stare at me. "No, I'm not."

I cocked my head and grinned at him. "I bet you I can change that," I said, and then leaned over to kiss him.

At first, it was like crashing against a solid wall. But then he gave way, and his lips became frantic against mine. He jumped up from the chair and crushed me to him. When he finally jerked away, I panted for air. "That's more like it," I gasped.

He ran his fingers through his hair and then shook his head. "I can't do this, Jordan."

"I don't understand—"

"We can't see each other anymore. It was wrong, and it never should have happened."

I stared at him in disbelief, slowly shaking my head from side to side. It felt as if his lips were moving, but I couldn't make out what he was saying. "Not see each other anymore? But why?"

"You're too young. I took advantage of you."

I snorted. "Took advantage of me? Has there ever been a time I came to you unwilling? I've wanted you every time—I want you all the time."

He winced. "It doesn't matter. It was wrong."

Heat filled my cheeks as I tried desperately to fight for him, to fight for *us*. "But I don't understand. Why would you suddenly decide it was wrong?"

"I'm trying to make things work with my wife, Jordan. She doesn't know about you, but she knows I've been having an affair."

"Why did you tell her?"

"I didn't. It all came out in therapy."

My eyebrows shot up in surprise. "Therapy?"

He nodded. "I—well she and I—have been in couple's counseling for a long time."

"For what?"

He gazed down at the floor. "Well, if you must know—"

"I think I have a right to know if you're blowing me off!" I cried, bringing my hands to my hips.

Coach T raised his gaze to stare me straight on. "For sex addiction."

I gasped.

"Anyway, I love her, and I want to save my marriage."

My heart skidded to a stop, and I fought to find my breath. "But…I-I love you," I protested.

51

"No, you don't. You just think it's love."

"Now you're telling me what I feel?" I shook my head. "I've never loved anyone in my life the way I've loved you. These past few months have been the best months of my life. I want to be with you." My arms encircled his neck. "Forget about your wife. She doesn't make you happy. I can see that. You know I can make you happy. I'd do anything for you, I swear!"

He took my arms and pulled them away. "In time, you'll see this is the right thing. You need to be with someone your own age. You'd realize in a few years that you didn't love me, and it was all just a crush."

My chest felt like it was caving in. I couldn't believe the same man who couldn't get enough of me just three days ago was now blowing me off, reducing my feelings to nothing more than fucking puppy love.

Tears stung my eyes. "No, it's not a crush."

"Jordan—"

"So was I just some piece of young ass to you?" That thought burned in my mind. Was I just a conquest to him? Something he did to see if he could get away with it? Part of his alleged sex addiction? After all, guys usually only wanted me for one thing. And once they used me, they tossed me aside. The sad thing was I never seemed to learn.

I stared pleadingly into his eyes, waiting for his response. He sighed and brushed a tear off my cheek. "No, you weren't. You are much, much more to me, I promise. And I do care for you."

"Care for me? I tell you I love you and I want to spend my life with you, and you can only say that you *care* for me." My mind spun with what he had told me earlier about his wife knowing he was having an affair. "Is there someone else?"

He refused to meet my gaze.

Then out of the corner of my eye, I saw a speck of blue peeking out of the couch cushion. That one tiny piece of cloth sent electricity firing through me and an image formed in my mind. "So you swear that there isn't someone else?"

"No, of course not."

My head shook maniacally as I stalked over to the couch. I ripped out the fabric, which happened to be a pair of panties with white embroidery reading *Captain*. "Then what in the hell is this?"

The color drained slowly out of Coach T's usually tanned face. He looked like a corpse standing in front of me. And then I remembered Melanie streaking across the parking lot, and it hit me. "You're doing Melanie, aren't you?"

He stared at me in disbelief. "Jordan—"

Fury crashed over me. I'd been replaced by Miss Goody Two-Shoes! I struck out at him as best I could. "She's your son's girlfriend, you pervert!"

"It's not like that at all."

"Oh, and why did she leave here just a few minutes ago looking like hell?"

"If you would calm down for a minute, I would explain!" He reached out his hand for me, but I jerked away.

"I sure hope you can because you're gonna have a hell of a lot of explaining to do when I go to Micheltree's office in the morning!"

I clamped my mouth shut, regretting what I had said. But in spite of the acid nature of my words, Coach T's reaction was not what I expected. Instead of a face filled with fear, he stared mockingly at me. "Go ahead and tell your little story. No one will believe you."

"What?"

"Think about it, Jordan. I'm a well respected teacher with tenure in the county." He jerked his head toward his Victory Wall of trophies, plaques, and awards. "Not to mention, I've got one of the best coaching records around. I'm practically a god around here. And then there's you: someone who is a known liar who has been a frequent resident in detention for cheating, skipping school, and other offences." He stared daggers at me. "Who do you think they're going to believe?"

I trembled under his glare. I'd never seen this side of him before. He'd always teased me, joked with me...been tender with me. This was frightening.

But I refused to let him see how scared I was. "You don't know what they'll believe."

His lips curled into a cruel smirk. "Well, I guess we'll just have to see."

I stared at him in shock before flinging the panties at him. My hair fell in front of my face, shielding the tears that flowed. Slamming his office door, I stalked out of the gym and into the icy night.

My mascara stung my eyes and blinded me, causing me to stumble towards my car. Thoughts swarmed in my head like an angry beehive. *This can't be happening. He'll come after me. He'll realize he's wrong. He doesn't want me to tell. He LOVES me.*

I slammed the car door and banged my head on the steering wheel. Without bothering to cover my mouth, I screamed and thrashed and sobbed. My vision became clouded by a mixture of eyeliner, mascara, and salt.

I'd been rejected.

Again.

I glanced at my reflection in the mirror. He was going to pay. I was going to hurt him like he'd hurt me. If it was the last thing I did, he would pay.

* * *

My mother has never been a cookie-making, PTA Mom. She had me at twenty, and I guess you could say we grew up together, especially after my dad took off when I was five. From that moment on, it was Mom and me against the world.

So, I knew when I entered the house, crushed and sobbing, she would be on my side. It wouldn't matter that a married man had broken my heart—a married man who was a coach and teacher at my school. The details would be insignificant compared to the fact I was in pain.

Since it was late, I knew she would be doing her second favorite thing—working out. I descended the stairs to the basement as loud 80's music blared in my ears. Mom seemed to only be able to get her exercise groove on to the big hair bands. As my hand hovered over the doorknob, I could hear the faint humming noise of the elliptical.

Once I opened that door and spilled my guts, there would be no turning back. Secrets spoken out loud could never be silenced. They always seemed to spiral out of control, filling you with regret that you ever acknowledged them.

I was right. The instant Mom saw my tear stained face, she gasped. "JoJo, what's wrong?" she asked, hopping off the machine. She was at my side at an instant.

"Oh, Mom, it's so awful!" I cried, sinking down on the exercise bench.

She brushed the hair away from my face. "Tell me what happened."

Slowly, I purged myself of mine and Coach T's affair. It was like I had word vomit and couldn't stop. I related every intimate detail, every stolen moment together. Mom sat like a statue by my side, never reacting, never gasping with horror or disappointment. I had to say I was pretty impressed she didn't go on a profanity filled tirade.

When I finally finished, Mom stared at me wide-eyed. "Oh, JoJo, I'm so sorry!" She pulled me into her arms. "Who does that son of a bitch think he is? Tossing you aside like a piece of shit!"

"I know," I moaned. For a fleeting moment, I felt comforted by her rocking me back and forth.

Mom's breath echoed in my ear. "Don't you worry, baby. He's not going to get away with this. We're going to see that he pays."

"No, you don't understand. When I told him I would tell about the affair, he mocked me. He said no one would believe me over him because of my reputation." I shook my head and wiped my eyes. "Maybe he's right. Maybe no one will take my word over his."

Mom took my hands in hers. "It's all about your story. You're just a kid—he took advantage of you. He basically raped you." When I started to protest, Mom held up her hand. "This is what has to be done. Now think. There must be something you have on him— something he can't dispute."

56

"Like what?"

Mom rolled her eyes. "Intimate stuff, JoJo. Like if he's not circumcised or if he has a tattoo or a scar somewhere only you would know about."

Frantically, I searched my mind for any incriminating details. Then an image formed in my mind. It was this past New Year's Eve night. Coach T's wife and Will remained out of state for the holidays. He'd come back early—claiming just to be with me.

After we rang in the New Year with champagne and strawberries, we lay intertwined in his bed. I tried ignoring his wedding picture staring at me from the dresser. Instead, I focused on him. "What's this?" I asked, as I playfully traced a scar running the length of his hip. I'd felt it several times before, but I'd never thought to ask. It had rough, jagged edges, but in the middle, it was smooth to the touch.

"Oh that?" He asked, peering down at his hip. "That's my gang wound."

I cocked my eyebrows at him. "Bullshit! You're too much a pansy to have ever been in a gang!"

Coach T laughed. "I didn't say I was in a gang. I said it was a gang *wound*."

"Uh-huh," I murmured, propping my head on my elbows to stare at him.

"Yeah, this one time when I was in college at Northwestern, I passed by this basketball court where all these gang members were playing. Being the cocky asshole I was, I strode out there and challenged them to a game."

I rolled my eyes. "You're still a cocky asshole."

"Will you let me finish my story?" he asked, a grin hovering at his lips.

"Fine, fine."

"So I beat one of their star players, this huge guy covered in tattoos. So he's all pissed and needing to save face, so he pulls a knife on me. Cuts me from here to here," he took my hand in his and rubbed my fingertips along the scar. "Sixty stitches later, I have a battle wound that never goes away."

"Poor baby," I said, bringing my lips to his. "A couple of more inches, and you would have been in real trouble."

"Umm, hmm," he murmured before pushing me back down on the bed.

I jolted out of the vision. I stared at Mom before blurting, "He has a scar."

Mom nodded. "Good, good. Where is it?" She closed her eyes and said, "Please tell me it's somewhere incriminating, somewhere not everyone can see!"

"It's on the inside of his hip down to his groin."

"Nice! Oh yeah, that one's gonna come back to bite his ass!" She practically clapped her hands together with glee.

But I didn't share her excitement. Something about all of it made me uneasy. I nervously chewed my lip before saying, "Mom, I'm not so sure about accusing him of rape."

"You're already eighteen, Jo-Jo, so a consensual affair isn't going to do very much to hurt him. But," she paused, "if it's rape, we can ensure that he really pays for how he took advantage of you both with his teaching career and maybe even jail-time." She then nonchalantly untied her dark hair. It cascaded down her back before she tossed it absentmindedly over her shoulder. She acted like I'd just said I wasn't sure what I should have for dinner, not that I wasn't sure whether I should frame the coach who'd dumped me.

I sighed. "I want to hurt him, but..."

"But what?" she demanded.

"I-I...love him."

Mom shot up from the workout bench. "Jordan, what have I told you about men and love?"

"You never, *ever* fall in love with them," I recited, like an obedient child. Hell, I knew it by heart. She'd ingrained it in me since I was twelve years old. Normal moms encourage their daughters to fall in love and to experience romance. But not my mom.

She nodded in approval. "And why do you never fall in love with a man?"

"Mom, please—"

"Say it, Jordan!"

I glared up at her. "As long as man has your heart, he controls you!"

"That's right. And you don't ever want to be controlled by a man. *You* want to control *him*."

"I know, I know," I protested feebly. "I didn't mean for it to happen. It just did."

She smirked at me. "And look what it got you. Tossed aside so he can move on the next piece of ass." Rolling her eyes, she murmured under her breath, "Just like your father."

I cringed. It never failed whenever some guy had screwed me over that Mom managed to mention my dad. Somehow I seemed to be paying for his sins with every relationship or hook-up. "Okay, okay. I'm sorry. I want him to pay for what he did."

Mom cocked a dark eyebrow at me. "Are you sure?"

"Yes."

59

"Because you've got to be absolutely certain of your decision before we go forward. There's no going back once you accuse him."

I refused to meet her expectant gaze. Instead, I stared down at my hands. "Yeah, I'm positive."

Mom's nails dug into my chin as she jerked my face to hers. "Dammit, JoJo, I mean it. I'm not going to bat for you if you're not certain you want to see that asshole pay."

Swatting her hand away, I stared coldly at her. "I said I was sure. What the fuck do you want me to do? Write it in blood?"

Mom smiled. "There's my fiery girl. You had me worried there for a minute. You're going to need that fire in you if we're going to make this happen."

Rolling my eyes, I spat, "Just get off my back and stop worrying about me, okay? I'll do what I have to do. I'll even ham it up and cry while I describe how he threw me down and raped me." I brought my hands to my temples. My head had begun pounding.

"So?" Mom asked.

"*So*, I'm going upstairs to take some Advil before going to bed and putting an end to this truly screwed up day!"

Mom shook her head. "Not before we get your story straight."

"You mean sit down and go through it like we're writing a damn novel or something?"

"Yes, that's exactly what I mean. You gotta march into that principal's office tomorrow with a story no one can poke holes into."

I stared at her for a minute. "Do you realize how seriously fucked up you sound right now?"

She laughed. "Oh honey, this is nothing!" She motioned around the room. "Do you think we'd have all of this if I wasn't totally fucked up?"

Chapter Six: *Jordan*

I didn't make it to bed until close to midnight. We talked everything through a million times. No detail was spared as Mom and I fabricated the story of how Coach T had raped me. In the end, it wasn't hard since he had taken advantage of me along with taking what little trust I had left in men. Every time I started to falter on my feelings about crying rape, I thought of the way he had acted in his office—how he was probably doing Melanie behind my back. That caused the anger to pulse in my veins, and I wanted him punished.

The next morning I barely touched my breakfast. My stomach churned so tightly in knots I felt like I would throw up. *Get a grip, Jordan! You're acting like some pussy about this. Get your head on straight and your act together.*

Mom drove me to school. From time to time, she would turn to look at me. Each time, she flashed me a winning smile. "It's gonna be okay, JoJo. You'll see," she reassured.

To keep my focus, I once again kept my mind on how he had treated me the night before—the things he'd said, the look of hatred he'd given me. That was the Coach T I wanted to pay. I locked the other one— the one I truly loved—out of my mind.

I strode confidently through the office door with Mom close on my heels. I stopped at the secretary's desk. "Yes, I need to see Dr. Micheltree."

The secretary, who was a floater and sometimes substitute teacher, eyed me disdainfully before staring down at an appointment book in front of her. I guess she remembered subbing for some of my classes. I fought the urge to laugh in her face about how ridiculous she was to hold a grudge over stupid shit like that. But I refrained.

"Do you have an appointment?"

"No, I don't."

A shit eaten grin spread across her face. "Oh, I'm sorry then, but Dr. Micheltree won't see you unless you have an appointment. You'll have to come back."

I opened my mouth to make a smartass remark, but Mom pushed me aside. She leaned in on the counter—her face inches from the secretary's. "Now you listen to me. I didn't haul ass all the way down here to be told to come back some other time. I should be at work right now, and I don't intend to come back. So, we'll just have a seat until she can see us!"

Without another word, Mom turned on her heels and clicked over to the couch. She shot the secretary one last angry look before she flounced down. I stood rooted to the floor, almost as astonished at the secretary, whose mouth still hung open wide. But then, I went to sit down beside her.

Barely five minutes had passed when the secretary cleared her throat. "Dr. Micheltree can see you now."

Mom threw a triumphant glance at me before rising from the sofa. "Thank you so much for all your help," she drawled in a sugary, sweet voice as we passed the desk. We wound around through a circle of offices before arriving at Dr. Micheltree's door. Mom knocked.

"Come in," a voice called.

We walked in the office. Mrs. Tillery, Dr. Micheltree's secretary, smiled at us. "She just stepped out. Please have a seat, and she'll be right with you."

We eased down in the leather bound chairs in front of the desk. "Have you ever been in here?" Mom asked, in a whisper once Mrs. Tillery left the room.

"Nope. Just Mr. Sands office."

"I see."

Dr. Micheltree didn't keep us long. She breezed into the office, her usual dark bob bouncing. "Good morning," she said, with a smile. I couldn't help but wonder how fake she seemed. I guess she was used to putting on a front for irate parents. "And what is it you've come to see me about?"

Mom cleared her throat. "I'm Ms. Bradford, and my daughter, Jordan, has something she needs to tell you."

I stared at Mom in disbelief. I never imagined her throwing me under the bus in the first two seconds, but she had. Maybe even a small part of me hoped she would say the words—that she would utter the lie that had to be spoken. But she didn't.

Dr. Micheltree looked expectantly at me. "Yes, Jordan?"

This was it—the big moment. The invisible line drawn in the sand that I had to cross. I swallowed nervously before I finally found my voice. "I was raped."

Dr. Micheltree's eyebrows shot up and disappeared into her forehead. "Here on campus?"

I nodded.

She stared at me in shock. "I'm so sorry, Jordan. When did it happen?"

"Last night."

"And where was it?"

"The gym."

I held my breath, waiting for her to ask the one question she seemed to have forgotten. She knew when and where, but she seemed unconcerned with who it was. I mean, wouldn't you think it would be the most important question? It sure as hell would be to me. But the truth was, she was more concerned with her precious school's appearance—like who could get their ass in a sling because they weren't properly supervising students.

Her brows furrowed together, and she finally asked, "Do you know who it was?"

"Yes."

"Who?" she prompted.

I glanced over at Mom. She bobbed her head in encouragement. I looked back at Dr. Micheltree. "It was Coach Thompson."

I expected a range of reactions from her—shock, disbelief, horror, outrage…anything but what she said was certainly not one of them. "You must be mistaken."

The wind left my body in one long whoosh. "Excuse me?" I croaked.

She avoided my gaze by staring down at her lap. "I said, you must be mistaken. Mark Thompson is one of the finest teachers we have here at Newton. His reputation is impeccable."

Before I could argue with her, Mom leaned forward in her chair. "Just what are you trying to say?"

Dr. Micheltree clasped her hands together. "I feel that perhaps your daughter is mistaken."

Mom's face reddened. "You think she's mistaken about being raped? And just how does one go about being mistaken about something like that?"

"I just feel she needs to be careful who she is accusing."

Anger washed over me. I heard Coach T's voice in my ear. *"Go ahead and go to the office. They won't believe you...."*

"You think I'm lying, don't you?" I demanded.

Dr. Micheltree refused to answer. "One second please. I want to call Mr. Sands in here. He's an Assistant Principal as well as our athletic director."

"I'm not lying!" I shouted.

She held her hand up to silence me. "Just a moment, Jordan."

Within a few seconds, I heard Mr. Sands name being paged over the intercom. He must've been close by because he appeared in the doorway just a few minutes later.

He didn't seem too surprised to see me. After all, wasn't I the badass with a reputation and record? "Hello Jordan," he said, pleasantly.

"Hi," I grumbled. I'd gotten to know Mr. Sands fairly well in the four years I'd been at Newton. He was my administrator so whenever I got written up for doing something, I had to go to him for my punishment. In all those years and through all the shit I'd done, we'd had plenty of opportunities to strengthen our relationship.

He walked over to have a seat next to Dr. Micheltree's desk. "Just what seems to be the problem?"

"Jordan wants to make a rape claim against Mark Thompson."

66

The color drained from Mr. Sands' face. "Excuse me?"

I nodded. "He raped me Monday night in his office."

Mr. Sands gave me a sad look. "Jordan, do you know what you're saying?"

"Yes, I do!" I snapped. Their doubt in my credibility was seriously pissing me off. Regardless of what Coach T had threatened, I never imagined *I* would be questioned. I thought it would all be him. "Why would I lie about something like this?"

Mr. Sands glanced over at Dr. Micheltree, and she gave a short nod of her head. "Jordan," he began, "you do understand the seriousness of the accusation you are making. Whether guilty or not, educators never recover their reputations after something like this happens." He paused and drew in a deep breath. "I know that teachers can sometimes be unfair and make students angry. Sometimes they can get so angry over an F on a paper or a snide remark they decide they want to make a teacher pay. This isn't what this is about, is it?"

I smirked at him and fought the urge to shout, *"This isn't about some stupid F or a smart ass remark! It's about him screwing me for three months and then dumping me for no apparent reason!"*

But I didn't. I merely shook my head from side to side. "No, Mr. Sands, this isn't about revenge. I was raped."

He leaned forward in his chair. "Jordan, I've known you for the last four years. In that time period, you've managed to stay in trouble fairly consistently."

I snorted. "So?"

"Just try to hear me out, okay? I mean, here we've got you, a student who has been known to cheat on tests and lie about her whereabouts when skipping class. Then we've got a coach like Mark Thompson. He's been teaching for fifteen years without blemish or complaint. Never has a girl come forward in all those years with such an accusation." He shook his head. "Who would you believe?"

Once again Coach T's words echoed through my mind. I clenched my teeth and growled, "I was raped!"

Mom sighed in exasperation. "JoJo, give the doubters your evidence. Maybe then they'll eat their words."

Dr. Micheltree and Mr. Sands both stared expectantly at me. I suppose they were waiting for me to whip out a soiled pair of panties or something with conclusive DNA evidence.

"Coach T has a scar on his right hip. It runs from his pelvis down to his inner groin."

The room grew eerily silent. It felt like all the air had been sucked out. Dr. Micheltree leaned back in her chair, unable to speak. Mr. Sands stared down at the floor. Neither one of them would look at me. They both acted like I was some diseased element on their picture- perfect campus.

It pissed me off.

I crossed my arms over my chest. "Did you hear me?"

"Yes, Jordan. We heard you," Dr. Micheltree said softly. When she looked up at me, hurt pooled in her eyes. But it wasn't hurt for me. I could read it so easily I almost bolted from my seat to slap her.

It was all for Coach T.

Since they didn't have any sympathy for me, I decided to give them something I'd even held back from Mom—something that would really make them hate Coach T. "He did it to Melanie Reeves too! I found her panties in his office futon!"

Everyone's heads swiveled to stare at me. Even Mom's expression changed to horror, but I think it was because she was afraid I had just overplayed my hand. When she recovered, she cleared her throat. "So, now that you see the truth, what are you going to do about it?"

Dr. Micheltree exchanged a glance with Mr. Sands. "We've never had an accusation of this kind here at Newton. It's unprecedented."

Mom rolled her eyes. "That's all well and good, but I want to know what you're going to do to the son of a bitch?"

"There's protocol already in order, Ms. Bradford, of what we are to do. We must call the Sheriff's department. Jordan will have to be interviewed and then—"

I sat up in my chair. "What happens to Coach T while all this is going on?"

"Until formal charges are brought against him, he'll continue working at the school."

I gasped, and Mom grabbed my hand. "You mean to tell me he can commit rape and walk the halls a free man?" she asked.

Dr. Micheletree nodded. "Only until formal charges are filed. I'm sure the Sheriff's Department will expedite the situation."

"Well then, I suppose we need to get to the Sheriff's Department right now then?" Mom asked, picking up her purse.

"I suppose so."

Mom motioned for me to stand up. Dr. Micheltree and Mr. Sands didn't look pleased we were leaving. I figured the sooner we went to the authorities, the sooner their perfect school was wrecked.

We'd almost reached the door when Dr. Micheltree cleared her throat. "Ms. Bradford," she began. Mom and I turned back to look at her. "I do hope we can keep this as quiet and as uncomplicated as possible."

I cringed as Mom shuddered by my side. I braced myself for what she was about to say. She flashed Dr. Micheltree a winning smile. "Of course. I'll be happy to keep it as uncomplicated as coaches who can't keep their dicks in their pants!"

And with that, she slammed the office door behind us.

Chapter Seven: *Melanie*

I didn't sleep at all on Monday night. After I woke up a little after two to find Will gone, I couldn't go back to sleep. For the rest of the night, I lay in bed, staring at the ceiling. Both an emotional and physical ache rippled through my body. And even though I wanted to sob with despair, I couldn't cry. I was eerily calm while over and over like a movie on repeat, I relived what had happened in Coach T's office.

At six-thirty, Mom came bustling in to wake me. "How are you feeling, honey?" she asked, sporting her pink flowered robe.

"I'm okay," I lied. It was pretty sad how good I was becoming at bending the truth. The Old Melanie was literally disgusted by it. But lying not only preserved my sanity, but it insured my survival. And no matter what, I had to survive.

"Were you able to sleep last night?"

I shook my head. "I think I'll stay at home and take it easy today."

The truth was I just couldn't face Coach T yet. Not only would I run the chance of seeing him during school, but I would definitely have to see him at practice. The thoughts of walking past his office to get to the locker room caused my stomach to lurch and churn.

"That's probably best. I'll go bring you some breakfast before I leave for work."

"Thanks, Mom."

She kissed the top of my head before heading on to wake my younger brother, Luke.

When Mom came back an hour later, she brought me breakfast and some Advil. As she started to leave, she turned back to me with a smile. "Now try to get some rest today. And don't you worry a thing about basketball. I just got off the phone with Coach T, and he told me to tell you not to come in to practice."

The Advil lodged in my throat. I gulped down the water before I looked at Mom. "Y-You talked to him?" I couldn't bring myself to speak his name.

She nodded as she absentmindedly smoothed my rumpled sheets. "I didn't want you to get in any trouble for missing practice. You know how ridiculous he can be about that."

"Yeah." Coach T often joked that the only reason to miss practice was for a death in the family—and that was your own.

Mom smiled. "I think he feels just awful about what happened."

My chest heaved, and I fought to find my voice. "What do you mean?"

"Well, I think he feels he's to blame—you know for asking you to go get that silly pump. I assured him it could've happened to anyone and not to blame himself." She glanced up at me. "Melly, you look so pale! If you're not better this afternoon, you're going to the emergency room, young lady. No ifs, ands, or buts!"

My mouth had gone dry. "Okay, Mom."

"That's my girl." She came back over and kissed me on the top of my head. "See you tonight."

I nodded and forced a smile. But as soon as I heard the garage door slam, I sank back into bed. The thin

72

veil holding my emotions in check ripped in two. Pulling the covers over me, I was finally able to cry again. Desperate sobs rolled through me as my emotions raged like a storm, shaking my body so hard the bed creaked and groaned beneath me.

Once I finished crying, my thoughts turned over like a switch, and I seared with white hot anger. I began screaming and thrashing like a two-year-old throwing a tantrum. The range of extreme emotions frightened me.

Finally, I was spent. Exhausted and hoarse, I tried catching my breath. It came in short, sniffling hiccups. As I lay there with my arm draped over my eyes, I thought about Coach T. I wondered if he was glad I wasn't going to be at school or practice, or if he worried that my avoiding him meant my resolve was breaking. But knowing him, he probably wasn't worried about me telling. After all, he could prey not only on using Will against me, but the shy part of my personality that would loathe the attention that coming forward would bring. He had me trapped in more ways than one.

Even if he knew I wouldn't tell, I wondered if he was worried about facing me again. Like me, did he worry what he would say when he was around me? Or how he would act? Did he wonder how he could possibly stand next to me and act like everything was all right?

The thought overwhelmed me, causing my breath to quicken into anxiety-ridden pants. But thankfully and mercifully, I fell into a deep sleep.

* * *

Sleep on Tuesday turned into a self-induced coma. I barely woke up long enough to speak to Mom and curl my nose up in disgust at the offer of food. I slipped in and out of consciousness—in and out of the nightmare that had taken over my life. Light turned to dark and then turned to light again.

Wednesday dawned, and I knew whether I wanted to or not, I had to go to school. It wasn't just about facing my fears, but it was more about getting Mom off my back. I didn't want her hovering around me, worrying that the bump on my head was the cause of my problems. As long as she was around me, I was afraid I might blurt out the truth.

As I rolled out of bed, I grabbed my cell phone. I glanced down at it and groaned. I had a million new text messages. I imagined they were from Lauren and other team members, and there were probably some from Will. Just the thought of scrolling through them overwhelmed me, so I just turned my phone off.

I didn't bother fixing up. After I showered, I pulled my hair into a ponytail. I slipped on a pair of jeans and team hoodie. When I got downstairs, I found the kitchen empty. Luke had early practice this morning, so Mom had left to take him. I grabbed a piece of toast and a water bottle and headed out the door.

As I drove to school, everything seemed the same as it had before—the same traffic, the same early morning radio station's corny jokes, the same morning parking lot antics at school. The world had kept right on turning despite what had happened to me.

But everything normal changed when I entered school. I heard it the moment I pushed through the double doors into the front lobby. It was a slow whine like an annoying gnat interrupting a picnic. The kind you couldn't drive away by furiously swatting your hands.

As I started down the blue and white tiled hallway, it became a low rumble—ominous and dark like a storm brewing on the horizon. I glanced at the faces around me, my heart thudding to a stop. The usual goofy grins and wide-eyes of gossipers had been replaced by masks of shock and horror.

My first thoughts were that someone had been killed. The air constricted in my lungs. It was the same somber atmosphere as two years ago when a popular junior died in a car accident. Who could it have been? Suddenly Will's face flashed before my eyes.

Oh, please, God. Not Will!

But as I passed by each buzzing group, conversation silenced. I bit my lip and shifted my book bag that suddenly felt like lead on my shoulder. It took only a second for me to realize that a death wouldn't silence conversation. No, that kind of swarming hum was reserved for rumor and accusation. Someone was in trouble. And then I knew.

The masks of horror were for me.

Numerous pairs of eyes burned through me, questioning, judging, mocking. At that moment, I would have done anything to escape—sold my soul if I had to. The slow burn on my face crept down my neck, and I began to wonder if it would spread out onto my arms as well.

There's no way they know. Only you and Coach T know what happened, and there's no way in Hell he's told! As much as I tried to calm myself down, it didn't help very much. My heart continued pounding. *Just let me make it to my first period class.* But when I hurried around the corner, I skidded to a stop. Dr. Micheltree and two men stood outside the classroom.

Suddenly, I forgot how to breathe. A voice in my head screamed, *"In and out, in and out!"* Picking up my feet seemed foreign, and if someone hadn't bumped into me, I would have been forever cemented in that spot.

When they saw me, Dr. Micheltree started forward, parting the crowd like Moses with the Red Sea.

"Melanie, will you come with us please?"

Speaking was not even a possibility. Fear wound tightly around my vocal cords, restricting my air. I merely nodded. I followed her and the men back down the hallway.

The looks were even more intense now. I made the mistake of glancing up once, but after the expressions on people's faces, I ducked my head back down again.

They don't know. They don't know. They don't know! Once again I rationalized that only Coach T and I knew, and he would never, *ever* tell. He had sworn me to secrecy, hadn't he? There were no cameras in the gym, and no one had been left at school that late besides us. No one could know!

As much as I tried believing that, I couldn't possibly understand why I was being summoned to the office not two days after what had happened, nor why everyone looked at me like I was diseased or something.

I was thankful when Dr. Micheltree ushered me into the main office. It was virtually empty this time of the morning, so there was no one else to stare at me. The clicking of her heels echoed off the tile floors as we made our way down the long corridor to her office.

When we got inside, she motioned for me to have a seat. I eased down in the leather chair, never taking my eyes off of the two men in suits.

They must've noticed my apprehension because they smiled. The tallest one stepped forward and extended his hand. "Melanie, my name is Jay Pendley. And my partner is Lewis McKay." He paused for me to shake both of their hands. "We're investigators with the SVU of the Sheriff's Department."

My heart pounded in my ears. "SVU? Like the television show?"

Detective Pendley laughed. "Yes, I suppose so. We're here to investigate a claim of sexual misconduct."

"S-Sexual misconduct?" I repeated, lamely. *Don't let your voice crack, Mel.* Then the familiar Miranda rights echoed in my head... *Anything you say or do can be used against you in a court of law.*

"Yes, by one of the coaches here at the school," Detective McKay replied.

I glanced across the desk at Dr. Micheltree. She briefly met my gaze before averting her eyes to her desk calendar. *Keep yourself together. Don't blush, don't stutter, don't give them anything.*

I played dumb as best I could. "Um, who are you supposed to be investigating?"

Detective McKay exchanged a glance with Detective Pendley. There was so much eye-shifting and strange looks it made my skin crawl. Finally, he spoke. "Mark Thompson."

I jolted back in my seat like I had been stunned with a taser. *Oh God, they know. How do they do possibly know?*

At my reaction, Detective Pendley nodded. "I know it probably sounds unbelievable at the moment, but we do have some evidence to back it up."

Evidence? What kind of evidence could they possibly have? Pictures, video, an eyewitness? "But what does this have to do with me?" *Give them something good, Mel. Push the heat off you anyway you can.* I gasped and brought my hand to my chest almost theatrically. "Did one of the other players accuse him of something?"

"No, it wasn't one of the other players." Detective Pendley hesitated. He looked over at Detective McKay who nodded. "It was Jordan Solano."

I was stunned. It took a moment for me to even put a name with a face. Suddenly, a scene flashed before my eyes. It was of Jordan and Coach T at the ball game a few weeks ago. Plainly, I could see her flirting with him, but I also saw the look of amusement on his face. He certainly wasn't reciprocating her advances. I couldn't imagine why she would lie about such a thing.

I shook my head at the officers. In a voice that didn't sound like my own, I blurted, "Coach T would never do something like that."

"Melanie, we—"

For Will and for my fractured sanity, I continued coming to Coach T's defense. "She's lying. I know she is."

"That's a pretty hefty claim," Officer McKay countered.

"But I know her. Jordan's always in trouble. And when she's not in trouble, she's lying to get herself out of trouble. Don't you know she's a slut!"

"Melanie!" Dr. Micheltree admonished.

I couldn't blame her shock. I acted like someone even I didn't recognize. The Old Melanie would have never thought of calling someone a slut in front of the principal. I would have blushed and died a thousand deaths. But the Old Melanie was dead—staked through the heart on an old futon in Coach T's office.

So, the New Melanie shrugged my shoulders in total apathy. "Well, she is."

Detective Pendley shook his head. "Ms. Solano's character outside of this investigation is not our concern."

"But how can it not be?" I protested. "I watch enough TV to know that an accuser's character is always taken into consideration." When they didn't respond, I continued on, "I know she had crush on Coach T, and she flirted with him all the time. But I know he would never have acted on it." *Right, Mel. He's one hell of a stand up guy. He doesn't hit it with the flirty slut. Oh, no, he just rapes his star player on the futon in his office.*

Detective Pendley held up his hand. "Melanie, there's more."

I shifted nervously in my seat. "More?"

He nodded. "Yes. Ms. Solano alleges there was another victim."

"Who?"

Detective Pendley cocked his eyebrows. "You."

The wind left my body, and I wheezed. Detective McKay stepped forward, but I shook my head. Slowly, I tried calming myself down. *Breath Melanie! In and out, in and out, in and out.* Finally, my voice came back to me. "She said he…" I couldn't even utter the word. I thought if I said it, then it might make it true. Worse, it might give away my secret. The one I clung to so viciously it hurt.

Keep calm, don't freak out! Frantically, I searched my mind for answers. There's no way she could know. There were no windows in the office, so she couldn't have seen what happened. But why? Why was she saying that? What could she possibly gain by telling such a thing about me?

Detective McKay nodded in response to my last question.

Heat radiated through my face all the way down to my neck. I burned so hot I felt like I was on fire. I imagined flames licking at my arms and legs, scarring me physically like the ones I carried on the inside. *Stop it. They're watching you. Tell them something, anything, so they'll stop staring at you.*

Thankfully the New Melanie took over. I threw my shoulders back. "That's crazy! Why would she tell such a lie?"

Detective Pendley stepped forward. "Is it a lie, Ms. Reeves?"

My mouth gaped open. *Keep it together, Mel. Don't let him in. Don't let him see through to the truth.* "How can you even ask such a thing?"

"You didn't answer the question," he pressed.

Rage like I had never known spilled out of me. I bolted up out of my seat. "Yes! Yes, of course it's a lie! Coach T would never do that to me!"

Screaming those words was almost liberating—like I really could pretend it never happened. *That's right. He would never do that to you. You don't have to believe it, think it, or feel it because there was no way it happened.*

Before I could say anything else, I heard a commotion outside of the door. There were raised voices out in the hallway, and I could hear Mrs. Tillery, Dr. Micheltree's secretary, arguing with somebody. She wasn't successful because without even a knock, the door blew open.

Then my parents burst into the office.

"Excuse me, this is a closed meeting--," Detective McKay began, but my dad stopped him.

He pointed his finger in McKay's face and shook his head. "Oh, no, this isn't a closed meeting. That's my daughter you're interrogating right now, and she has right to counsel!"

My face flushed. Leave it to my dad to go full on lawyer mode. "Dad," I began.

"And if you think you're gonna ask her one more thing without counsel, you got another thing coming!"

"Daddy," I said.

"She's seventeen years old. What could she have possibly done?"

"Sir, she hasn't-" Detective Pendley started before Dad interrupted him again to continue on his tirade.

"She's an A student, Captain of the Varsity Basketball Team, and a Who's Who in American High Schools—"

"DAD!" I shouted.

Finally, he glanced over at me. "Please calm down. My rights haven't been violated!"

He raised his eyebrows, and I nodded. He then sighed and backed out of McKay's face.

"Please, Mr. and Mrs. Reeves. Have a seat," Dr. Micheltree said

Mom eased down into one of the chairs, but Dad kept pacing around the room.

"Can someone please tell me what is going on? I mean, my wife and I get a call to get down here immediately since our daughter is being interrogated by detectives from the Sheriff's department, not to mention the deluge of calls we've received from other basketball parents about something with Coach Thompson."

Detective McKay stepped forward. "Your daughter has been named as a victim in an investigation of sexual misconduct, Mr. Reeves."

Mom gasped, and Dad's face reddened. "Excuse me?"

And there they were. The looks I'd imagined—the looks I had feared—were etched across my parents' faces. I had to do something, so I blurted, "It's not true!"

My parents ignored me. "What do you mean sexual misconduct?" Mom asked, her voice wavering.

"We've had allegations that Coach Thompson raped a student here. When she came forward, she gave your daughter's name as another victim," Detective Pendley replied.

Mom slowly shook her head in shock. "Mark Thompson a rapist? I can't believe it," she said in a hushed voice

Dad grunted. "Well, I *don't* believe it. We've known him since Melanie was a Freshman. There's no way in hell he could have done anything to anyone, least of all Melanie!"

My face flushed with heat again, and I stared down at my hands. Their response was something I never expected. No arguments, no need to be convinced by me that it wasn't true. Just an open and shut case of the unwavering innocence of Coach T. It was at that moment I knew there was no going back. If my own parents found it so appalling, how would I ever convince anyone it was true?

Detective McKay sighed. "Look, I understand your frustration and disbelief, but we've had an allegation of misconduct. We have to investigate it to the best of our ability."

It was then a thought popped into my mind, and I blurted, "What's going to happen to Coach T?"

Dr. Micheltree finally spoke up. "He's been put on leave pending the investigation."

The news sent the Old Melanie kicking into high gear. My eyes widened in shock. "But you can't do that! We still have five games left in the season, and we're undefeated. Coach T has to be there for us when we go to the playoffs."

Once again, I didn't think about me. Just like I'd put Will first and then my parents, I put my team's happiness above my own. The reason seemed obvious enough to me. They were like my family. We would be broken without Coach T.

Dr. Micheltree shook her head. "I'm sorry, Melanie. We had no choice. We will have to pull Coach Simms up from JV to take his place or something. We haven't had a chance to figure that all out yet."

Tears of frustration stung my eyes. "It's so unfair." *Good God. Did you really just say that? Do you honestly think so highly of the man who raped you two nights ago? You are seriously losing it.*

Detective Pendley cleared his throat. "We will need to question Melanie further. I know this has been a great shock to her today, so I'd like to wait until tomorrow to do that. It isn't necessary, but you might want to obtain an attorney for the hearing."

Dad nodded and mumbled he would ask one of his partners. But I ignored him. All I focused on was 'hearing'. "You mean, I'll have to go to court?" I asked.

Detective McKay nodded. "Yes. If what you say is true, that Coach Thompson never raped you, then you will have to testify under oath."

I started to feel shaky. Testifying meant talking in front of a crowd of people. A crowd who would all be staring at me. And all of it under oath and on the record. I would be lying under oath, which from my Government class I knew was a felony. I could perjure myself.

But how would I even get that far. First of all, they'd put a Bible in front me. A Bible I would be forced to swear on that I would tell the truth, the whole truth, and nothing but the truth so help me God. Even though I was in a crisis of faith, I still didn't think I had it within me to swear on a Bible and lie.

It was all too much.

I needed out. I didn't want to be closed up in that room with them anymore. I frantically searched for an escape. I was slowly unraveling, and I needed time to regroup.

When I rose from the chair, my knees almost buckled underneath me. "C-Can I go now?"

"Sweetie, are you sure you want to go back to class?" Mom asked.

Dr. Micheltree nodded. "Your mom is right, Melanie. I'm afraid by now, word has spread throughout the school about what's happened. It might be better if you went home and took it easy today."

After experiencing what I had earlier in the day, leaving school was a tempting thought. But one person's face flashed before me.

Will.

Pain radiated through my chest at the thought of what he must be feeling or going through—if he was even here at school today.

I glanced at the faces peering expectantly at me. I shook my head. "If I did that, then everyone would think I'd bailed because it was true." *But it is true. You were raped, Mel.* I jerked my chin up. "No, I want to go to class. I want to be with my friends." *Why? So you can become exhausted by keeping up your little façade that nothing happened? So you can reassure each and every one of them it isn't possible Coach T raped you when you know good and well he did?*

Mom exchanged a look with Dad, and he nodded. "I suppose it's all right if you stay."

"Thanks." I gathered up my purse and backpack.

Mom hopped up and hugged me. "It's going to be all right, sweetie." In her comforting embrace, I almost believed her. But deep down I knew it wouldn't. Too much had happened for things to ever be all right.

"Thanks, Mom," I murmured.

Before I could make it to the door, Dad stepped forward and hugged me, too. *Oh Daddy, I wish for just one instant you could have wrapped your mind around it, considered it, contemplated it. I'm not your little girl anymore. You'd kill him if you knew the truth. You wouldn't stand here and defend him. You'd break his neck.* "Call us if you need us. I'll call Garrison when I leave here to represent you," he said.

I nodded. "Okay then."

Detective Pendley stood in my path. "Ms. Reeves, we'll need to talk with you tomorrow morning. Is nine am all right?"

No! No, it's not all right. I don't ever want to see you again, least of all talk to you! You'll keep on and on until you break me to get the truth. Before I could respond, Dad said, "If it's feasible with her attorney."

Detective Pendley nodded. I didn't say anything else as I sidestepped past him out the door. I blushed at the looks the secretaries gave me. "Melanie, do you need a pass?" Mrs. Tillery asked.

Staring out the glass office, I saw the bell ending first period had just rung, and the halls were crowded.

"No, thank you. I'll be fine."

"All right. Have a good day."

"Thanks," I mumbled.

Even though I kept my head down in the hallway, I could feel the looks burning into me. I quickened my pace, desperate to make it to the gym. At the mere thoughts of walking through those doors, my chest tightened. There would be no Coach T there. For four years I depended on him as part of my day. I was guaranteed to find him dribbling basketballs balls or setting up the volleyball net.

But he wouldn't be there today. He wouldn't be grinning and joking with the other coaches. He wouldn't be there to tease me or ride me about missing an easy shot.

Bitter tears stung my eyes. *You're so stupid, Mel. Did you honestly think it would ever be the same? That you could just walk back in those doors like you did on Monday and pretend that it never happened?* I was almost to the gym door when someone caught me by the arm.

It was Will.

"I need to talk to you," he whispered.

I didn't bother arguing. Instead, I let him lead me past the gym out the back door to the parking lot. We stopped when we got behind the field house.

I dropped my book bag and purse and stared expectantly at him. When I did, I gasped. I'd never seen him so shaken. His body trembled, and his face was ashen. His emotional pain crushed him physically. And that broke my heart.

He stood with his lip quivering like he wanted to say something but couldn't.

"Will?"

Finally, he lowered his head. "Is what they're saying about my…" he choked on the words.

No, please don't ask that. Ask me anything else. Ask me about the weather or how many shots I'm averaging a game.

I had to think fast. His gaze burned into my face. Once again, I vied for a Best Actress Academy Award. I gasped and reached out for him. "No, no, of course not!"

Tears of relief shimmered in his eyes. "Really?"

In the last forty-eight hours, I had never wanted to tell someone so much as I did at that moment. The words scorched my tongue. All I had to do was open my mouth, and they would tumble out.

But I didn't.

Instead, I kept my mouth firmly shut and nodded. He exhaled slowly before pulling me into his arms. His breath warmed my neck against the cold. "Thank God. I don't know what I would have done if it had been true." He kissed the top of my head. "I would have died, I guess. I couldn't have lived with myself if Dad had done that to you."

A sob caught in my throat at his words. Of course, he would have died. How does one survive the news your father raped your girlfriend? Your heart would stop instantly, and no matter how many people pumped up and down on your chest or how many times they shocked you back, you wouldn't survive. How could you?

But in the same token, I wondered how *I* was still standing. Why wasn't I six feet under from the shock of what had happened? How was I living, breathing, and lying like nothing had happened? Part of me might have been living, but the other part of me wished I was dead. I shuddered at the thought. I closed my eyes and pressed myself closer to Will. For the first time all morning, I felt safe.

He sighed, this time his breath warmed my ear. "I feel like a real prick for even thinking it. I mean, he's my dad. I shouldn't have even questioned it."

No, Will, your dad is the prick. I pulled away to stare into his eyes. "Don't blame yourself. It's only natural for you to question it."

"I mean, when I heard it was Jordan, I didn't believe it. I know what kinda girl she is, and I've seen the way she struts her ass in front him." He angrily shook his head.

I nodded. "I can't believe they took her word. I tried telling the detectives today what kind of girl she is."

Will's face softened. "You took up for him?"

"Of course I did. He's been my coach for four years." I paused and drew in a deep breath. "And he's your dad."

Tears welled in Will's eyes. "You don't know what it did to me when they mentioned your name. When they said, he'd..." he shut his eyes before he continued. "that he'd raped you, too."

"Will, don't," I urged.

He opened his eyes. "I-I didn't want to even imagine it."

Neither do I. That's why I'm lying—for you and for me. I brought my hand to his cheek. "I'm sorry you had to hear it from the gossipers."

"I didn't hear it from them...I heard it from the police."

My hand jerked away to rest over my mouth. "What?"

He nodded. "They read off the charges when they came to arrest him."

"They actually arrested him?"

Will leaned back against the field house wall. "Yeah, with handcuffs, reading his rights, and putting him into the back of the police car in front of all the neighbors leaving for work."

I shook my head. "Will that's awful." I tried drowning out the voice screaming in my mind. *Are you crazy? He deserved it! Hell, he even deserves to be gang raped over and over in prison for what he did to you!*

"It was."

Without another word, I reached out and wrapped him in my arms. "I'm so sorry." I rubbed my hands over his back in wide circles. "I love you, Will. I know it's a stupid thing to say right now, but I want you to know how very much I love you."

He pulled away to kiss me tenderly on the lips. "I love you, too, Mel. More than anything in the world."

89

He wound his fingers through my hair. "I don't know what I would do without you. My dad feels the same way."

Saliva rushed into my mouth, and I feared I would vomit. Instinctively, my hand flew to my mouth. "Are you okay?" Will asked.

I nodded. In barely audible voice, I said, "He doesn't think I said anything, does he?"

Will shook his head. "No, he knows that it was Jordan who made the accusations. When he heard your name, he shook his head and said, 'She'll testify for me'."

BASTARD, the voice screamed in my mind. *That fucking bastard! He knows what he did to me! He knows what he took, and he expects me to testify for him? Because of my love for Will, he's using me like I'm just a pawn in his game.* My chest tightened. *But this isn't about him, remember? It's about the boy you love who holds you right now. It's about protecting everything you hold sacred.* I wrapped my arms tighter around Will. He laughed. "Hey now, you're gonna squeeze me to death if you don't stop!"

"I'm sorry. I only feel safe when I'm in your arms."

He smiled. "Don't be sorry. You squeeze me all you want then. It feels pretty damn good to me too."

I stared into his dark eyes. "What are we going to do, Will?"

"We're going to stay strong. The hearing will be in a few weeks. You'll testify that Jordan lied about you being…" Will stopped abruptly, unable to repeat the word.

I nodded. "Yes, yes, of course, I will."

"Once the judge hears the evidence, he'll throw the case out the window. I mean, Jordan's been in trouble most of her life. Hell, she's probably been before most of the judges here in town."

"Yeah, that's true."

Will brought his lips to mine. "It's going to be all right, Mel. As long as we're together, we'll get through it."

"I know, Will. You're all that matters to me."

"But there's something else right?"

I sighed. "Everyone was staring at me this morning. I know it's only going to get worse." Tears welled in my eyes. "And the team. What will they think about me when I show up for practice?"

"They know you, Mel. Once you tell them it's all a lie, they'll understand."

No, it's more like once I lie. I'll only be a part of the team if I lie. I can only keep Will if I lie. I can only keep my sanity if I lie. "You think it'll really be that easy?"

"Yep."

Finally, I smiled. "This isn't supposed to be the way it goes. I'm supposed to be comforting and reassuring you instead of you reassuring me."

Will laughed. "We're here for each other, remember? I'm all right, and you're all right."

"We're all right," I said, softly.

"Exactly."

I glanced back at the building. "Don't you think we ought to head back?"

He made a face. "What excuse are we gonna give them for being late to class?"

"We can say we got called up to the office."

"Yeah, that sounds good. I mean, I'm sure they know what's going on, so they probably won't question us."

91

I picked up my purse and book bag and followed Will back into the building. After being with him, I felt revived—at least for the moment.

Chapter Eight: *Jordan*

Thursday I faced the firing squad by going back to school. I'd spent all of Tuesday afternoon with Detectives Pendley and McKay of the SUV unit as well as Mom's lawyer. When I was told that Coach T would probably be arrested Wednesday morning, I decided I better stay home. I turned my cell phone off, and I didn't take any calls on my home phone either.

So as I headed back to school, I was a little nervous. It was pretty much a guarantee that gossip had fanned through the entire school the day before. Even though I wouldn't have to face Coach T, there was the rest of the student body, including Melanie, to contend with.

I eased my black BMW into a spot. It was five minutes until the bell rang, and everyone hurried into the school. I sucked in a deep breath before grabbing up my purse and book bag. Like I'd done years before in beauty pageants, I pulled my shoulders back, jerked my chin up, and walked into the building with my head held high.

My stoic front didn't last long. I'd barely gotten past the front office before someone bumped into me. "Hey, watch it!" I cried.

"Lying bitch," the girl murmured under her breath.

"Screw you," I called over my shoulder.

I started towards my locker. I couldn't ignore the looks of hatred people gave me, nor the comments people made as they passed me. But I kept right walking as if nothing had happened.

When I got to my locker, I gasped. Scraped into the metal was the word, "WHORE". Beneath it was "LIAR".

Conversation silenced around me. Everyone stood stock still, waiting for my reaction. Tears stung my eyes. But I wouldn't let them see me cry. I whirled on my heels and started back down the hall.

I barely made it in the bathroom before I started crying. I locked myself into the handicap stall and sobbed. It wasn't supposed to be like this. I was supposed to make *him* pay. I wasn't supposed to get punished too! I mean, why were they doing this to me? Didn't they know what he did to me? That he'd used me and just threw me aside?

The sound of the door opening silenced my tears. I stood up and wiped my eyes. When I heard the stall close next to me, I walked outside. I glanced at myself in the mirror and groaned. My face was all splotchy, and mascara stained my cheeks.

I bent over the sink and washed my face. As I patted it dry with a paper towel, the stall opened.

It was Melanie.

When she saw it was me, she gasped. She started for the door, but I stopped her.

She ducked her head and stared down at her shoes. "Let me go," she protested in a whisper.

"I know what happened."

She jerked her head up to stare at me. "You don't know anything but lies! I mean, it's one thing for you to pretend you were raped, but I don't know why you needed to drag me into it!"

I narrowed my eyes at her. "If it's nothing but lies, how come I found *your* panties in *his* futon cushions?"

Her body tensed, and I wanted to laugh at her. I mean, only Melanie could be "Miss Priss" and get uncomfortable with the mention of her underwear. "I don't know what you're talking about."

"Your panties with the word "Captain" embroidered on them."

The color drained from her face. She swayed back and forth, and for a minute, I thought she might pass out. Her body trembled all over like a leaf, and because of how green she looked, I fought the urge to back up just in case she hurled or something. But she also looked like she was concocting a reply in her mind. Then like in a truly bipolar moment, she shook her head. "I don't care what you say. Maybe it was my underwear. Maybe it fell out of my bag after practice, did you think about that?"

When I saw she wasn't going to throw up, I leaned forward. "He was playing us, Melanie. Don't you see that?"

A sad expression crossed her face. "You really had an affair with him, didn't you?"

"What if I did? What if I slept with him for three months before he tossed me aside? And what if I wanted to make him pay for hurting me? Maybe you ought to consider punishing him too!"

"But I wasn't having an affair with him!" she protested, but her resolve deflated. Instead of the steely bitch she was just a second before, she seemed broken. Her lip quivered, and she appeared on the verge of tears. So maybe she wasn't having an affair with him. It was kind of a long shot to begin with. I mean, why would she be interested in Coach T when she had Will aka Mr. Perfect all to herself?

But then a revelation came crashing down on me. The harshness of it was so fierce I was the one trembling instead of Melanie. My memory flashed back to her Monday night in the parking lot with her messed up hair and smeared makeup. They weren't willingly hitting it in his office. He hadn't turned me away that night because he had been with someone.

Oh, no, it was much worse than that.

I stared at her in disbelief. He had screwed her—the panties were proof of that. But it wasn't by her consent…he had truly raped her.

I gasped. "Oh my God!" My mind shattered with the thoughts of what he had done. To his star…to his *son's* girlfriend. It was too much. I slammed back against the sink and shook my head. "He raped you, didn't he?"

Her eyes widened in horror. "NO!" she screamed.

I couldn't believe she was in complete and total denial. "It's true, isn't it?"

Melanie head shook back and forth so fast she looked like someone twitching with Parkinson's disease. "Stop saying that! He didn't do anything to me!"

"I was waiting for him in the parking lot Monday night. I saw you leave the school after everybody else. I saw how you looked!"

"No, no, no! I'd been running and sweating at practice."

I couldn't believe she was still denying it. I would have wanted him to fry if he'd really raped me. Why would she want him to get away with it? "Why are you lying for him?"

"I'm not!"

I reached out and grabbed her arm. "You have to tell the truth, Melanie. You have to make him pay for what he's done."

She slung her arm away. "Stop it! He *didn't* do anything to me. You're just a spiteful slut who shouldn't have been sleeping with a married man."

Before I could respond, Lauren burst through the door. Her eyes narrowed at me. "What the hell are you doing? Isn't it enough you gotta lie about Coach T, but now you're harassing, Mel? Jesus, you're pathetic!"

I jerked back like I had been slapped. "You don't know what you're talking about!"

"Whatever." She turned to Melanie. "Come on, Mel. Let's go."

"You better tell the truth!" I cried, as Lauren put her arm around Melanie and led her out of the bathroom.

My fingers dug into the sides of the sink. As I thought about Coach T raping Melanie, I fought my gag reflex. What kind of unimaginable bastard was he? How could I have possibly loved someone who would do such a vile and disgusting thing?

I flung my head back and stared back at my reflection. It was all such a fucking mess.

* * *

At lunch time, I headed to my usual table. Tara and Brandi were already there, but the rest of our crew was missing. It had been two days since I'd seen them. Tara had called and left several messages, but I didn't return them. I knew she wanted to talk about Coach T and what I'd accused him of. But I didn't want to talk about it with her. Somehow I was afraid if I did, she might break me down and get the truth out of me.

I eased down into a seat. "Hey guys."

"Hey," Tara said softly.

When Brandi didn't respond, I stared up from my lunch-bag. She glared at me, her green eyes narrowed. "What?" I finally asked.

She shook her head in disgust. "You know what."

"Um, no, I don't. So why don't you save me the trouble," I countered.

"You and your Coach T story."

"It's not a story."

Brandi snorted. "Yeah, it is. I saw how you used to flirt with him, how you looked at him. You *wanted* him."

"Yeah, I may have flirted him, but I sure as hell didn't want him to rape me!"

"He's a good man—he's a married man!"

"You're just pissed because he's your darling Will's father, and if he's in trouble or hurt, Will's hurt. You're pathetic."

The venom rolled off my tongue before I could stop it. It was the only self-defense mechanism I knew— hurt others if they hurt you.

Brandi stared at me with a wounded expression before snapping up out of her chair like a rubber band. "Go to hell, you lying bitch!"

As she stalked away from the table, a couple of kids glanced in our direction. Wide-eyed, Tara shook her head. "What are you doing, Jordan?"

"What am *I* doing? She started it."

"That was low to bring up Will. You know how obsessed she is with him."

The expression on Tara's face broke me. "Okay, okay. I was a bitch. I'm sorry. It's just you have no idea what today has been like for me. People calling me names, my locker's been vandalized. Stupid me, I'd hoped my two best friends would be here to support me—not give me shit the moment I sat down."

Tara refused to look at me. "You have no idea what it's been like for us either."

"Excuse me?" I asked.

"You weren't here yesterday when the shit hit the fan, Jordan. Brandi and I were the ones getting the looks and being pushed and shoved in the hall. And for what reason? Simply because we're your friends."

I chewed on my lip, unsure of what to say. "I didn't know—"

"Maybe you would have if you'd bothered to answer your phone last night!"

"I'm sorry, Tara. I mean, I was in with the detectives all yesterday. I was worn out and didn't want to talk to anybody, okay?"

She shook her head. "I had a right to hear it from you, Jordan."

"I know you did. And I'm sorry. I'm really, really sorry."

"I hope you are. We're been best friends since third grade. I would hope you'd feel I had a right to know what was going on with you—especially something as serious as being raped."

"You *are* my best friend, and yes, you had a right to know. I made a mistake. I promise it won't happen again."

Tara sighed. "You promise?"

"Yes, I promise."

She fidgeted with the buttons on her sleeve before sucking in a deep breath. "Jordan, I want to ask you something, and I want you to give me an honest answer."

My mind spun with her question. *No, Tara. Not you. Please don't make me do this. Don't make me lie to your face.* But I didn't give in to my emotions. Instead, I angrily shook my head. "Don't you start this bullshit too!"

"I know how you felt about Coach T. You told me one time that you loved him, remember?"

"Yeah, and if memory serves me right, I also remember being drunk off my ass!"

Tara's eyes flashed. "Don't try to blame it on alcohol. You sobbed for an hour and told me how much you loved him."

My throat went dry. I swallowed several times before I shrugged nonchalantly, as if she didn't have me cornered with my lies. "So, maybe I did like him. And maybe because I was drunk, I exaggerated how much I liked him. But that doesn't mean I wanted him to rape me!"

Tara pushed her lunch bag aside and leaned in on her elbows. "Tell me the truth."

"He raped me," I insisted.

"I'm your best friend. If you can't tell me the truth, how can I be your friend?"

My heart beat rapidly in my chest. I wanted so much to tell Tara the truth—to tell someone what had really happened besides my Mom, but I couldn't. There was too much risk. So, I forced the lie from my lips one last time. "I was raped."

Tara stared at me, her mouth hanging open in astonishment. Then she silently gathered up her things.

"Wait, don't leave!" I cried.

"Did you not hear anything I just said? If you keep lying to me, I'm not your friend anymore, Jordan. When you decide to tell the truth, you come and find me."

And with that, she stalked away from the table, leaving me all alone. I sat in shock for a few seconds, trying to gather my thoughts. Then I realized what it must look like for me to be sitting by myself. So, I gathered my things and started out of the lunchroom.

There was really nowhere for me to go. I couldn't go out to the sunshine of the courtyard. I would be in the same situation. No one wanted to have anything to do with me. As I cast my eyes toward the library, I realized that wasn't an option either. You had to get passes in the morning to go there.

Finally, I took my things and started for the parking lot. For the remaining thirty minutes of my lunch, I sat in my car, my coat pulled around my shoulders, and my iPod plugged in my ear. I didn't listen to my usual rap or pop playlists. Instead, I listened to classical music in a desperate attempt to drown out my problems.

It didn't work.

Chapter Nine: *Melanie*

After my horrific run-in with Jordan, I spent the rest of the school day in a fog. I went through the motions, going to class, taking notes, poking the food on my lunch tray, but my mind was miles and miles away. Now I had the answer to why she had claimed I was raped. She'd found my panties and thought I'd been voluntarily sleeping with Coach T. The very thought made me shudder with disgust.

Somehow she, of all people, had seen through my lies. I'd been so convincing to everyone else, even the detectives.

But not Jordan.

With one expression, she saw through to my core and knew I had really been raped. Knowing that someone else knew the truth was emotionally crippling. I could only hope that because of Jordan's reputation that no one would believe her, and they would continue believing my lies.

When the bell rang, I silently rejoiced. I wanted nothing more than to get home and bury myself under the covers again. But when I got to my locker, Will was waiting on me. "Ready to go?"

My brows furrowed. "Go where?"

"To the Circle of course," Will replied, giving me a funny look. The Circle was a spot in the athletic park below school where our gang of friends hung out. The gang was comprised of juniors and seniors, athletes and non-athletes. It didn't matter if it was warm weather or cold. With tail gates lowered and hatch backs raised, we would lounge around listening to music and talking.

But today when Will and I got there, it was different. An unspeakable tension hung around us, strangling our usual free flowing conversation. Plus, the very reason we were able to meet at this time of day was because Varsity basketball practice had been canceled—even the guys'. The coaches were spending an afternoon in meetings trying to sort out what was going to happen in Coach T's absence.

We shivered and huddled together in the winter cold. Finally, JT snorted exasperatedly. "Dude, this is bullshit!"

Will raised his head. "What do you mean?"

"I mean, we're all sitting here like somebody died over some rumor that bitch of a skank started!"

"Stop talking shit, JT," Lauren warned.

"I'm not talking shit. I'm stating facts," he argued.

Lauren tossed her strawberry blond hair over her shoulder and raised her eyebrows. "Oh really? Well, it sure sounds like shit to me. We're sitting here like somebody died because they did. Coach T's reputation and possibly his career."

"Lauren!" Breanna Perkins snapped. She jerked her blonde head towards Will and me. At the mention of his dad, Will stiffened at my side. I squeezed his hand reassuringly.

Lauren's face turned the color of her hair. "I'm sorry guys," she mumbled.

JT patted her on the back before glancing around at the rest of us. "Look, she's right in a way. I mean, we gotta man up here. Coach T is innocent. There ain't no way in hell he would've raped Jordan or…" He refused to meet my gaze. "Or anyone else for that matter."

His words stung me. My parents hadn't challenged the idea and now my friends weren't either. Kids I'd known for years, even my best friend, jumped to Coach T's defense without even a second thought. But in the end, I had done the same thing, hadn't I?

Breanna nodded. "JT's right. Just because they're accusing him doesn't mean he's going to jail. I mean, he's bound to be found innocent once we all testify."

Once they all testified…once they all unified together against me—against any of the truth I still harbored deep within me. My chest ached at the thought. I fought the urge to stand up and scream, *"It's the truth dammit! He really raped me, and you can all go to Hell for not believing it!"*

But I didn't.

Instead, Kara Ridings stood up to drive another nail into my coffin of truth. "I've known Coach T since middle school travel ball, and he's never looked at me or touched me in any way that wasn't totally appropriate!"

JT and Paul Jacobs grinned at each other. "Thank you, Kara. Save it for the detectives okay?" JT said.

She laughed. "Well, I was just saying, you know, that he's totally innocent."

"Seems like I remember a time when you and Jordan were BFFs," Lauren mused.

Kara rolled her eyes. "Please don't remind me!" She kicked a loose pebble with her shoe before climbing back on JT's truck bed. "Besides, that was before she was a sleazebag ho."

"She dated your brother, too, didn't she?" Breanna asked.

"Ugh, yes, on and off for like two years. Why, I don't know. Carson is the biggest asshole I know!"

Paul nodded his perfectly coiffed Afro while JT snorted. "Yeah, he is a pretty big asshole."

Through all the affirmations for his dad, Will remained silent. He stroked wide circles with his finger on my palm. I pulled my hand away and took his hand in mine. "It'll be fine," I murmured. I said it more for my own benefit than for his.

He stared into my eyes for an eternity before he finally smiled. "Yeah, I hope so."

Paul stood up. "Well, I say we do something besides sitting around on our asses."

Kara and Breanna exchanged glances. "And just what did you have in mind?" Breanna asked.

Paul shrugged. "I dunno. Something like a protest—you know, like in the 60's."

"Like a Coach T rally?" Kara asked.

JT nodded slowly before grinning. "Dude, that sounds like a hell of an idea!"

Through the hair shrouding my face, I peeked over at Will. His face lightened up instantly at the idea of a supportive rally for his dad.

"Okay, ace, where would we do it?" Lauren questioned.

"Like here at the school?" Paul suggested.

"Nah..." JT murmured.

Everyone fell silent for a minute then Paul snapped his fingers. "We could do it in front of the jail!"

I gasped. "The jail?"

He nodded as a big grin spread across his face. "Yeah, I mean, he hasn't gotten bonded out yet. And maybe he could hear us!"

It took a moment for it to sink in with everyone, but then they began talking at once.

"I bet we could get the news to come."

"We could start it at the school and drive in a caravan."

"And have posters and signs."

"I know my mom and dad would be in on it."

The voices blended around us like a hornet's nest of activity. Will squeezed my hand. His deep brown eyes had the first flicker of light in them since his dad had been arrested. It didn't matter how I felt that all my friends were organizing a protest in my rapist's honor. No, those thoughts were the farthest things from my mind. As long as Will was okay, I was okay.

* * *

By the next morning, word of the protest had grown to a frenzy. Once the booster club found out about it, they'd enacted the phone chain—the one usually only used in case of snow days or deaths in the family. It was truly something to behold. Every parent of a player had been called and sworn their allegiance to help in any way. Paul's dad even called all the local news stations and the newspapers.

Lauren organized a banner painting that afternoon after practice. Her mom and Breanna's mom were raiding Home Depot for paint, brushes, and signs while we were at school. Several other parents offered to buy pizza and drinks for all the workers. It sounded like it was going to be a fun time—at least whatever fun was supposed to be now, after everything that had happened to me.

That afternoon as I ran out of the locker room, my dad's partner, Garrison Michaels, stood outside the door, briefcase in hand. When he saw me, he stepped forward. "Melanie, we need to talk," he said sternly.

Lauren and Kara glanced at me before they ran to meet Coach Simms at half court. "Um, okay."

As I looked around for somewhere private, Garrison motioned to Coach T's office. "How about there?"

My stomach churned at the thought of being closed into the scene of the crime. But I managed to bob my head and follow Garrison. The moment the door closed behind us, tiny beads of sweat popped out on my forehead. The room never seemed so small, and I had to fight to keep breathing.

"Maybe you should sit down?" he suggested, motioning at the futon.

I stared at it in horror before turning my back to it. I took my anger out on Garrison by shooting him a seething look. Not only was I pissed that he had shown up at school, but I also didn't like his tone. "No, I'm fine. What is it?"

"I'm sorry I had to interrupt your practice like this, but we've got to set up a time to take your deposition."

"Oh, that."

Garrison nodded. "I wanted to try to give you some time to process everything that had happened. Since I was already here speaking to Dr. Micheltree, I thought I would catch you."

"When do you need me to do it?"

"As soon as possible. How about this evening after practice?"

I shook my head. "Tonight's really not a good time. You see I'm supposed to go help paint banners and signs for the protest we're having."

Garrison's expression darkened. "Yes, I heard about the protest."

"Can't I do it another time?"

He shook his head. "Melanie, there's another reason why I'm here besides the deposition. Earlier today, the DA brought forward some evidence in the case against Mark Thompson."

I fought hard not to pass out. "What kind of evidence?"

Garrison glanced down at his shoes. "Let's just say it's of a physical kind pertaining to Ms. Solano's case."

"Oh, I see," I replied, trying to hide my relief that they didn't have anything connected to me.

Clearing his throat, Garrison met my expectant gaze. "After hearing the evidence, your father and I feel it would be in your best interest not to attend the rally tomorrow."

"But why? You said the evidence belonged to Jordan's case, not mine. Coach T didn't do anything to me so why can't I go?"

"Melanie, when this evidence comes to light, it will prove without a shadow of a doubt that Mark Thompson was intimate with Jordan Solano—"

I gasped. So Jordan had been telling the truth when she admitted the affair to me in the bathroom. She really had slept with Coach T.

"Now whether it comes to pass that it was rape or consensual, we don't know right now. Because of what all that means to Mark Thompson's reputation, your father and I do not feel you should attend the protest."

"But I'm dating Coach T's son. Doesn't that already sully my reputation?"

Garrison sighed. "I'm sorry. That's our professional counsel."

"So does that mean I'm not supposed to go to the banner painting either?"

"Yes," he replied.

I threw up my hands. "I can't believe this!"

"Once again, I'm very sorry, Melanie. Perhaps it would have been better coming from your father."

"Whatever," I grumbled.

"Listen, I'll come by your house later this evening to take your statement."

"Fine." I brushed past him and ran out to the court. Coach Simms didn't bother riding me about being late. There would be no suicides for me since I was excused. But I hated being an exception. I would have rather taken the punishment and run until I puked.

Dread hovered over me at practice. I kept eyeing the scoreboard, waiting for Will to arrive for the boys' practice. It was the worst scrimmage of my entire career. I continuously missed shots and couldn't even connect with my teammates to see the ball down the court.

Finally, Coach Simms blew the whistle. "Reeves, over here!"

I pushed my sweat soaked bangs off of my forehead and trotted over to her. "Yeah, Coach?"

She stared me down. "Melanie, I've been making an exception for you because of what happened—"

I held up my hand to silence her. "You don't have to say anything. I suck today, but I would rather you call me out than let me ride on what I was doing because of what's going on."

Coach Simms pursed her lips and nodded. "All right then. Point taken. Here's what I think. You're done for the day. Go ahead and change. Make sure when you come back tomorrow that your head is outta your butt and on straight. Got it?"

I nodded. "Yes, Coach."

She smiled and then turned her back to me, giving her attention to the team—the ones who weren't total failures. I sprinted off the court into the locker room. I didn't change. Instead, I grabbed up my stuff and went outside to wait on Will.

I pushed through the double doors to find him and some of the guys sitting on a truck tailgate in the parking lot. The moment he saw me, his eyes lit up. He hopped down and jogged over to me.

"Hey beautiful," he said, planting a quick kiss on my lips.

"Hi," I said, my voice choked into a whisper.

He raised his eyebrows. "What's wrong? Is practice already over?"

I glanced past him to the guys talking and joking at the truck. "Um, no, it's not." I bit my lip. "Can we go somewhere to talk?"

"Yeah, sure."

Will led me around the side of the gym where we were alone. "What's wrong?"

"Garrison met me as I was coming out of the locker room."

"Oh?"

I shook my head. "I don't know how to tell you this, Will."

He reached out for me, his hands rubbing my arms. "It's all right, Mel. Whatever it is, just tell me."

"He says that I can't go to the protest tomorrow afternoon."

Will snatched his hands off me. "What? Why would he say something like that?"

I ducked my head. I didn't know how I was going to tell him about the evidence with Jordan. Stammering, I said, "H-He said t-there was some new evidence, and that because of all that I couldn't go."

"What kind of evidence?" Will demanded.

"Physical evidence tying Jordan and your dad together."

Will made a choking noise. "Are you serious?"

I nodded. "He wouldn't tell me exactly what it was, but he promised it would prove they had been...together."

For a moment, Will stood frozen like a statue. He didn't even blink. Tentatively, I reached out and took his hands in mine. "I'm sorry. I didn't want to have to tell you."

He shook his head. "No, I'd rather hear it from you than someone else." His eyes were a mixture of sadness and anger. "I just can't believe that there's some alleged evidence, and he was *really* with her. He swore to Mom and me he hadn't been with her."

"I'm so sorry," I murmured, squeezing his hands.

Will's dark eyes flashed for a moment, and his emotions turned over like flicking a switch. "Well, you're not going to listen to Garrison, right?"

Who was he kidding? In our entire relationship, I'd never stood up to an authority figure. It was probably one of the reasons I refused to stand up to Coach T about what he'd done. Finally I found my voice. "What do you mean?"

He leaned closer to me. "I mean, you're still coming to the rally, right?"

I stared pleadingly into his face. I didn't like how his emotions were yo-yoing out of control, but more than anything, I didn't like the hostility he directed at me. "Will, I just told you what Garrison said—"

"Yeah, and it's bullshit!" he snapped.

"No, it isn't," I countered softly.

Will raked his hand through his hair before he turned back to me. "Fuck whatever evidence they have. There's no way in hell my dad would rape anybody. Okay, so he might have screwed Jordan, and because of that, he had to lie to my mom and me about it. But no matter what, I know he didn't rape her."

There's no way in hell my dad would rape anybody. Those words stung me, and I fought to find my breath. When I didn't respond, Will grabbed me by the shoulders. "You're my girlfriend, Mel. I need you to support me and my dad."

"I want to be there, but I have to do what my dad and Garrison says."

"Look, I want you there at the rally with me tomorrow." His voice had a hardened edge to it, one like I'd never heard before, and it caused me to flinch.

"I've told you I can't. Why can't you understand?"

He shook his head. "Don't you see? If you're not there, everyone is going to think something is up. If they hear about the evidence and then not see you there, they're going to think all the rape rumors are true."

"No, they won't."

"Yes, they *will*." Even though he glared at me, I could see the tears shimmering in eyes. "Don't you want to be with me? Don't you want to support me?"

I fought the urge to shake him. I wanted to scream, *"Are you fucking kidding me? Do you even know what I'm putting myself through for you and for us? Not to mention lying about your precious rapist of a father!"*

Instead, I answered meekly, "Of course I do."

"Then come to the protest," he demanded.

"Maybe I can talk to my dad..."

"Fine." He started past me, but I grabbed his arm. "Will, please."

"I can't talk about this anymore, Melanie." He sighed. "And frankly, I can't be with someone who doesn't love me enough to stand up to her lawyer."

No, no, no! It wasn't possible he was giving me an ultimatum. Not after everything. And with his final words, he turned his back and stalked off toward the gym. I, on the other hand, remained rooted where I stood. My chest heaved, and I didn't bother fighting the sobs. They rolled through my chest with such force I had to brace myself against the building for support. But it became too much, and I slowly slid down the wall onto the cold concrete.

* * *

To say I was in a foul mood after practice would be a mild understatement. I refused to talk to anyone at dinner. Because of the way I'd reacted earlier, Garrison and Dad decided it would be better to wait until Friday to do my deposition. It was a good thing because I bolted from the table before anyone was finished. After escaping to my room, I changed into my pajamas and then pulled the covers over my head, trying to drown out the world. Everything was falling apart, and I didn't have the strength to pick up the pieces.

I was almost asleep when Mom rapped on my door. "What?" I demanded.

She poked her head in. "Melanie, are you all right?"

"I'm fine. I'm just tired."

I don't know why I bothered lying because Mom was used to deciphering my moods. She came over and eased down beside me on the bed. "What's wrong, sweetie?"

The feel of her hand on my hair sent me into desperate sobs. I fell into her arms and told her what had happened with Will.

"He can't really be mad over you doing what Daddy and Garrison told you to."

"But he is. You should have heard the things he said."

Mom smiled. "Honey, Will is going through an extremely difficult time right now. I'm sure the pressure is unbearable on him. After hearing about the evidence today, he probably just snapped. I'm sure he'll think differently tomorrow."

"You think so?"

"I really do."

I sighed. "But everyone is over at Lauren's tonight eating pizza and working on signs for the rally, and I'm stuck here. Why do I feel like I'm being punished for something I didn't do?"

Mom patted my cheek. "I'm sorry sweetheart." She glanced at the clock on the nightstand. Even though it was barely eight o'clock, she said, "Why don't you go ahead and get some sleep? You'll feel better in the morning."

I nodded. "Okay."

Mom kissed me on the cheek before leaning over to turn off the lamp. When she got to the door, she blew me another kiss and then shut the door.

* * *

I slept fitfully that night. Every hour I woke up to check my cell phone, desperate for a text from Will. But every hour I was disappointed, and by morning, my heart tightened so hard in my chest I could barely get out of bed to shower.

"What's the matter with you?" my brother, Luke, asked at breakfast.

"Nothing," I muttered, as I fought to get my cereal down.

"You look like shit!"

"Luke Alexander Reeves, your language!" Dad's voice boomed from the stove.

"Sorry," Luke mumbled, before going back to his bacon.

Later on the ride to school, he was relentless. "So do you look like shit because you and Will are fighting?"

I almost swerved off the road. "Who said we're fighting?"

Luke snorted. "Ethan Capanegro said that Will came into practice last night all pissed off. Some of the guys asked him what it was about, and he said you."

Heat radiated in my cheeks. I hated the fact my baby brother was in high school and privy to older friends who told him all of *my* business. Not that he probably wouldn't still hear it if he were in middle school.

But Luke seemed eager to know what was really bothering me, so I sighed. "He's mad because I won't go to the protest with him today."

He arched his eyebrows in surprise. "But I thought Dad and Garrison decided you couldn't go?"

"Yeah, that's right," I replied, as I eased into the parking lot.

"Well, he's just being a douche!"

I fought the urge to laugh in my brother's face. Trying to play it off, I merely shrugged. "Yeah, maybe he is."

After easing the car into a spot, I glanced over at Luke. His fits were balled up. "Luke?"

He turned to me. His dark eyes were fury-filled slits. "He just better not be talking shit about you today. I swear, if anyone talks shit about you, I'll punch his face in!"

"You don't mean that."

"Yeah, I do, Mel."

I shook my head. "Promise me you won't do something stupid that will get you in trouble?"

"Even if I was defending you?"

"You going to jail isn't going to make me feel better in the long run. So think with your head, not your fists."

He rolled his eyes. "That's so lame."

"Whatever. Just do it okay?"

"Yeah, yeah, I'll do it."

I smiled. "Thanks, bro."

Luke snorted. "Gah, Mel, quit being lame!" He grabbed up his book bag and practically sprinted away from me. That was Luke for you—one minute my knight in shining armor, and the next feeling like I was a dork of the highest caliber.

116

Something slammed against the glass of the car window, causing me to jump. It was Lauren and JT. "Hey guys," I said, as I climbed out of the car.

"You missed a good time last night," JT said.

Lauren punched his arm. "Dammit, I told you not to say anything. You know Melanie couldn't come."

"Geez, Lauren, lighten up on the roids, mkay?" JT joked, rubbing his arm.

I couldn't help but laugh. And for a moment, it actually felt good. There had been so little to laugh at lately that even one of JT's dumb jokes lightened my mood. We fell in line with the other kids streaming from the parking lot to the school. "Um, was Will okay last night?" I asked.

JT answered before Lauren could stop him. "Dude, he was in one pissy ass mood. I mean, he seemed all stoked we're doing the rally and all, but he acted like a complete dickhead."

Lauren rolled her eyes. "God JT!"

"What did I say now?"

She waved him dismissively with her hand. "Forget it. Come on, Mel, I'll walk you to your first period."

"Bye JT," I called over my shoulder.

I distinctly heard him grumble, "Women," before stalking away.

"You shouldn't be so hard on him," I said, as we worked our way through the crowd.

Lauren sighed. "The dude has no common sense, Mel. Did he need to alert you to the fact Will acted like a giant tool last night? Nope, I don't think so!"

I cringed. "He was really that bad?"

She nodded. "Yeah, he basically sat in the corner all night. He didn't paint, he didn't eat, he didn't do anything but just sit there and stare into space.

117

Everyone felt really sorry for him, but since I knew the truth, he's a giant asshole."

"Thanks, Lauren."

We hovered outside of my class. "So, has he called you?" she asked.

"Nope."

"Texted?"

I shook my head. "I don't know why he's being this way. I mean, it wasn't like I had a choice."

The bell rang, and she made a face. "Dammit, I gotta go. I'll meet you after, okay?"

"Sounds good."

As I walked past two of Will's teammates to my seat, they hushed their talking. They also refused to make eye contact with me. I guess Luke was right. Will had taken his anger at me out at practice, and now all the guys were pissed at me.

I remained in a fog all of first period. I could barely tell you what we even talked about. I hoped to be able to bum someone's notes later on. That was so unlike me. I was usually the one giving other slackers my notes. In the matter of a few days, my entire life had fallen apart. I barely recognized myself.

The bell rang, and I gratefully gathered up my books and ran for the door. I waited for Lauren, but she was nowhere in sight. Finally, I decided I'd better go on since I didn't want to be late. I was halfway down the hall when I ran into Will.

"Hi," I said.

"Hey," he mumbled, as he continued walking past.

"Will!"

He whirled around to give me an exasperated look. The annoyance gleaming in his eyes made my stomach churn. "Are you not even going to talk to me?"

"I said everything I needed to say last night. Either you're my girlfriend and you're with me this afternoon, or you're not."

And with those words, he turned on his heels and hurried down the hallway. I stood frozen, stung by his cold attitude and bitter words. I couldn't believe he was acting this way.

The bell rang over my head, but I never made it to 2nd period. Instead, I breezed right out the gym door and headed for the parking lot. When I got into my car, I texted Lauren and told her I was leaving school. I didn't call my parents or anyone else. I just drove home and climbed into my sanctuary and fell asleep.

Chapter Ten: *Jordan*

The rest of that Thursday back at school passed in a slow hell. Being treated like shit by the student body was one thing, but as the day wore on, I realized I had a new enemy—the teachers. Not that I'd ever been a teacher's pet or a great admirer of them. No, I already had a top spot on their shit lists. But there was a different feeling in the air. I'd taken out one of their own, and hatred for me simmered underneath the surface.

When I asked to go to the bathroom during fifth period, Mr. Guyer, one of the freshman basketball coaches, refused to answer or even look at me. Finally, I simply snatched up my stuff and stalked out. Let him write me up for skipping. I wanted to shout as I slammed the door, "I dare you to do it, asshole!"

The truth was I hadn't wanted to go to the bathroom. Instead, I wanted to clean out my locker. I knew I'd never let the jerks have the satisfaction of seeing me go to it again. Not with 'whore' and 'slut' gracing the outside.

Never in my life was I more thankful than when the bell rang at the end of the day. I headed straight for the parking lot since there was no one to stop and talk to. People avoided me like a wadded up piece of bloody tissue—including my two ex best friends. Even to the extent that kids crossed the halls to get away from me. Like brushing up against me equaled social suicide.

Yeah, screw you. I quickened my pace when I got outside. I just wanted out of there, to be home, to be away from the looks of hatred.

I slowed to a crawl at the sight of my car. "What the hell?" I cried. From the back fender to the front tail light ran a silver scratch. It wasn't just a quick slide either. Whoever did it took their time digging the key into the paint. I walked around to the other side where I found a matching scratch. Close to the back wheel was the world 'liar'.

I raised my eyes to see several kids staring at me. With a steely determination, I shouted, "What the fuck are you looking at?" They ducked their heads and continued walking. I threw my bags in the front seat and cranked my car.

When I left the parking lot, the tears flowed. It was all so unfair. The whole damn school acted like Coach T was some untouchable saint. And me, I was the villainous slut who ruined his good name. Because after all, no one knew the real truth. I'm sure they'd be singing another tune if they found out what the son of a bitch had done to Melanie. Yeah, it'd be a hell of a lot different then.

Even though I wanted to tell them to all kiss my ass, it wasn't that easy. In less than a week, everything I held dear had been stripped from me. The man that I loved, my friends, acceptance at school—it was all gone.

At work, I went through the motions like a zombie. I'd almost made it through the night when a table of four basketball players from one of the other county high schools sent me over the edge. They plopped down at a table in my station, outfitted in their practice uniforms.

When I walked up to take their order, I caught them snickering and elbowing each other. At first, I didn't think anything of it. I mean, it wasn't rocket science to imagine that once a night some sober or inebriated guy was gonna hit on me. I usually ignored them, and I could always rely on Marcus or Anthony to have my back if anyone got too physical.

"Jordan," one of the guys said—his voice low and husky. The way he said my name creeped me out. Like he was trying to be all seductive. Ugh. Not to mention he was stroking his upper-thigh when he said it. I fought the urge to slap him.

"Yeah, that's me."

"I'm Damon by the way."

I gave him a quick nod. "So what can I get you guys to drink?"

"We're not really thirsty, are we boys?"

"Nah," they agreed, snorting their laughter back.

My patience was wearing thin. Out of the corner of my eye, I searched for Marcus or Anthony. "Okay, then, what can I get you to eat?"

"We're *really* hungry," Damon drawled. "You know about being hungry, don't you Jordan?"

I narrowed my eyes at him. "Look, just cut the shit and tell me what you want to eat!"

He grinned wickedly. "I bet I know what you'd like to eat."

"Excuse me?"

"I like sausages, don't you? I bet you can't get enough of big, thick, manly sausages." His buddies snickered.

Crossing my arms over my chest, I shook my head. "Wow, I'm so impressed. Did you come up with that all on your own?"

"Tell me, Jordan. Do you just get your sausages from older men, or would one of us do?"

My breath hitched in my chest. "What did you say to me?"

Damon's fingers brushed across my thigh. "God, you must be hot for it all the time if you gotta get it from coaches too!"

Liquid fire shot through my veins. Before I could think better of it, I whirled around and grabbed the pitcher of ice water off the table behind me. "Go fuck yourself!" I screamed, as I dumped the pitcher of water on his crotch.

He bolted out of his seat, and I could only hope the stinging water pierced him like knives. "You bitch!"

Marcus appeared at my side, clenching his fists so his muscles bulged. "Is there a problem here?"

"Yeah, this bitch just poured water all over me!"

Marcus shook his head. "Nah, man. I think she was doing you a favor. I heard a little of what you were saying, and it seems to me that you've got a filthy mouth. I guess she was just trying to clean up your piece of shit ass!"

Damon stared at Marcus in shock. "Now you and your little bitches can get the hell out of here before I call the cops and file a sexual harassment claim on the four of you!"

The guys didn't argue. They followed Damon out of the restaurant.

My fury melted and left me stung and hurt by their words. Now my reputation and what had happened with Coach T had managed to spread to the other schools.

"Thanks, Marcus," I murmured.

"No problem, Jo."

"Can you tell Manny I'm gonna cut out a little early? I'll make it up tomorrow or this weekend."

He nodded. "Yeah sure." I started for the door, and he stopped me. "Listen Jo, I don't know what all happened at school and stuff. But I just want you to know that I'm here for you if you need me."

I smiled. "Thanks, Marcus. That means a lot." I leaned over and gave him a kiss on the cheek.

When I pulled away, he grinned. "No, *that* means a lot!"

I laughed. "Yeah, yeah, whatever."

It wasn't until I got into my car that I started crying. I cried all the way home. My mascara blinded me, and one time I almost hit a road sign.

After I pulled into the garage, I checked my appearance in the rear view mirror. I looked like a crazed raccoon with blackened cheeks. When I went inside, I found the house empty. A note on the counter told me Mom and her new boyfriend, Rob, had gone out for dinner. I sighed. Dinner could mean any number of things, and it usually meant she wouldn't come home all night.

I started upstairs to my room. The answering machine on the end table flashed new messages. As I began taking off my shirt, I pushed the button to play them back.

"Everyone knows you're a whore. You do anything that walks. You disgust me. I hope you rot in Hell for what you've done!"

The phone clicked off, and the machine played another message. *"You're a lying slut! I hope you go to jail instead of Coach T!"*

There came a shrill beep followed by another message. *"Listen bitch! You better stop lying about*

124

Coach T. *If you don't, you're gonna find yourself in a world of hurt! It's real hard to screw up people's lives when you're dead!"*

With trembling hands, I turned the machine off. I didn't want to hear anymore. Name calling was one thing, but now my life had been threatened.

Mom never came in that night, and I never went to sleep. I sat in the middle of my bed with her loaded .45 by my side until morning.

Chapter Eleven *Jordan*

I felt like the walking dead the next day. Third period rolled around, and I dreaded going to the gym. It had become a freaking shrine to Coach T—the place where his supporters made pilgrimages. Obviously, I wasn't a welcome visitor. I would have skipped out entirely, but I needed the credit to graduate.

I started into the locker room to change out when someone grabbed my arm. I shouted, both in fear and pain. Then I was dragged into the athletic room and thrown up against a rack of equipment. The metal cut into my back, and I screamed in agony.

In the middle of my scream, I heard the distinct sound of the lock clicking behind me. "Look, cut the shit and let me out. This isn't funny!" I growled, as I rubbed my throbbing back.

I heard someone reach for the lights. They flicked on, and I gasped. "W-What are you doing here?" I asked.

The imposing 6'3, two hundred pound form of Carson Ridings stared me down with his dark green eyes. He was Kara Riding's brother, but more importantly until Coach T, he was the only guy I had ever loved—or thought I'd loved. I'd lost my virginity to him when I was in the 8th grade, and he was in the 10th. When we were dating, I was too stupid and let him go off the deep end and slap me around. I'd dated him on and off for two years—until he left for college.

That's really when I began my pattern of dating guys who used and dumped me.

But it wasn't the presence of the former love of my life that scared me. It was the smoldering look of hatred etched across his face. I shuddered. "Answer my question."

He crossed the space between us in one long stride. Once again, he grabbed my arms. "I've heard the shit you're saying about Coach T."

I tried slinging away from him, but his grip was too tight. I knew if he didn't let go of me soon, I'd be bruised. But I kept my cool and jerked my chin up at him. "Yeah, so? What's it to you?"

At my response, he shoved me back into the shelf again, sending tears of pain to sting my eyes. "It's a hell of lot to me, you conniving little bitch!"

I narrowed my eyes. "Look, it isn't anything to you. We've been over for a long time now—even the random booty calls you threw my way have been long gone. So, the way I see it what happens to me is none of your damn business!"

Carson shook his head. "Listen to me. Through his Northwestern connections, Coach T has Kara a scholarship—a fucking full ride, you see? If he isn't here, she doesn't get the scholarship, and she doesn't go anywhere but maybe Harrison Community College."

"That's too bad."

Once again, metal cut into my back. This time I felt blood seeping through my shirt. "Stop it!" I cried.

"Not until you get it through your head, Jordan. My mom didn't fuck old guys to get rich like yours. My dad's disabled from that car accident, remember? He can never work again, and my mom is working two

127

jobs just to make it. Kara has busted her ass for four years, and she deserves that scholarship."

My chin trembled. "He raped me."

Carson momentarily released my arm. Before I could catch my breath, he sent a stinging slap across my cheek. "He never raped you."

"Y-Yes, h-he did!"

At my words, my other cheek rang with his slap. "He never raped you. I know you, Jordan. You screwed his brains out. I'm sure of that."

I shook so hard my knees threatened to give way. I leaned voluntarily against the shelves to keep my footing.

Carson jerked me forward. "Then what? He found someone else or he grew tired of your bullshit games just like every other guy." He snorted. "Jesus, you're pathetic!"

"Go to hell."

His hands tightened on my flesh. "Listen carefully to me. You're going to go to the authorities. You're going to tell them it was all a lie, and you're sorry. You're going to make things right, so Coach T can have his job back. Is that clear?"

"I'll never do that."

"Oh, yes you will," he countered.

"No, I won't! You can hit me all you want to. I was your girlfriend for two years, remember? I know what it's like to be knocked around by you."

Carson widened his eyes. "We're not talking about me. This is all about you!"

"Yeah, it is all about me. And I'm sticking to my story, and no one is going to make me change my mind!"

"Even if I promise you'll get hurt worse than any beating I ever gave you?"

Fighting the panicked sobs that threatened to break my sanity, I jerked my head up and stared coldly at him. Then I reared back and spit in his face.

He stared at me in astonishment. Before he could say or do anything, I said, "If you don't let go of me, I'll go straight to the police and press charges against you. Then your own precious scholarship would be in jeopardy!"

Slowly, his hands fell from my sides. "Bitch," he muttered under his breath.

I started towards the door. When my fingers grasped the doorknob, I turned back to him. "Don't expect me to feel sorry for you. We both know your old man was driving drunk when he had that accident. Driving drunk after meeting his mistress for a quickie at some seedy, out of town hotel."

His eyes glowed hatefully at me. "You shut your fucking mouth!"

Bolstered by the effect I was having on him, I cocked my head. "Can't handle the truth, Carson?" I paused as I collected myself. "I'm glad to see you're still as big a prick as ever. Beating up girls sure makes you a big man, doesn't it?"

With that, I spun around and unlocked the door. I couldn't get out of there fast enough. But I didn't go to the locker-room. Instead, I grabbed up my purse and book bag and headed for the hallway. I had just made it to the landing of the stairs when I felt the presence of someone behind me. But I never got a chance to react. Someone or something lunged at me, and I pitched forward, tumbling down the stairs. My head hit the concrete on the landing, and then everything went black around me.

* * *

As I started coming to, I had the worst out of body experience. My eyelids fluttered, taking in a small beam of light over my head. That beam of light caused me to panic since I thought it was *the light*, and I was dead.

But then I heard my mother's voice raging with profanity, and I knew I wasn't in the great light. When I tried moving my head, screaming pain seared through me, and I cried out.

"Jo-Jo?" A hand touched my cheek. "Oh honey, are you all right?" Mom asked.

"It hurts," I croaked.

Mom took my hand in hers. "I know, sweetie. You had a pretty bad fall."

"I did?"

"Yeah, some bastard pushed you down the stairs!"

It took a lot of effort to open my eyes. When I did, my mom gasped. "Would you look at the size of her pupils? I am going to sue this school for everything that it's worth!"

"Mrs. Solano—"

"That's Bradford," my mother corrected through clenched teeth. I fought the urge to roll my eyes. Of course, she would have to correct them. Even when I lay mangled and broken, there was no way in hell she wanted any connections to my father.

"My apologies, Ms. Bradford, but I can assure you there is no need to threaten us with lawsuits. What happened here was clearly an accident," a voice said on my right. I realized it was Mr. Sands.

130

Mom snorted contemptuously. "Pushing my daughter down a flight of fifteen stairs was no damn accident. Neither was defacing her locker and keying her car. But you people didn't take that seriously either."

This time it was Dr. Micheltree who responded. "Yes, we are taking it seriously, Ms. Bradford. We've been reviewing the tapes to find the culprit."

"Fantastic. I suppose you're going to do the same to see who it was who attacked her?"

I interrupted her. "I know who it was."

All the heads spun to stare at me in surprise. "But how could you possibly know, Jordan? I mean, from the tapes you were obviously pushed from behind," Mom argued.

"I still know who it was dammit!" I countered, trying to pull myself into a sitting position. When I heard the plastic paper crinkling beneath me, I realized I was in the bed at the nurse's office. Great, I didn't even want to begin to know how I got here. I imagined lying there in a crumpled heap for hours as numerous kids stepped over me. I'm sure it would make for some great gossip.

Mom reached out and helped me. Then she kissed my forehead. "Who was it baby?"

"Carson Ridings."

Dr. Micheltree and Mr. Sands exchanged a look. "But Carson Ridings doesn't even go here anymore. He graduated two years ago."

"Well, let's just say he decided to pay me a visit." With what little strength I had left, I raised my shirt out of my jeans. I gritted my teeth and twisted to the right.

At the sound of my mother's gasp, I knew they'd seen Carson's handiwork, and I slowly let the shirt fall. Then I fell back against the pillows, exhausted from that small exertion.

"So you're saying Carson came into school this morning and then assaulted you?" Dr. Micheltree asked.

I nodded.

"But why? Do you have a history with him?"

Before I could answer, Mom replied, "Unfortunately yes."

"Our history had nothing to do with today," I insisted.

Dr. Micheltree raised her eyebrows. "It doesn't?"

I shook my head, trying to find the words to explain why Carson had driven two hours from college to beat the shit out of me in an athletic closet in the gym.

"What was it about, JoJo?" Mom asked.

"Coach T," I murmured. I glanced at the others who peered anxiously at me. "He's angry about my accusations towards Coach T. Carson said without Coach T's connections, his sister wouldn't get the scholarship she needs. He wanted me to tell everyone I'd been lying."

Dr. Micheltree sighed. "I suppose this is a matter for the police, considering Mr. Ridings is no longer a student here."

Mom tossed her hair over her shoulder. "That's all well and good, but how do you propose to keep my daughter safe?"

Dr. Micheltree held up her hands. "Ms. Bradford we're trying our best—"

Mom strode across the tiny room to stand in front of Dr. Micheltree. "I'm sorry that I have to say you're doing a fucking miserable job, lady! I don't pay tax dollars to have my daughter bullied, beaten, and almost killed."

"Perhaps Newton isn't the best learning environment for Jordan at present," Mr. Sands said.

We all turned to look at him. He flushed a little before nervously clearing his throat. "What I meant to say is it might be in Jordan's best interest to transfer schools for a period of time. At least until things die down."

"And where would you suggest?" Mom asked.

"Pathways."

I gasped. "Are you crazy? I'm not going to that hell hole! Only druggies and bad asses go there." I stared helplessly at Mom. "I'm *not* one of those kids!"

"Jordan, lots of nice students go to Pathways. Some are merely academically behind, and they find the learning environment is more conducive to their needs," Dr. Micheltree said.

"Their needs? Like smoking pot or shooting up between classes?" I countered.

She grimaced. "No, that's not what I meant."

Before I could say anything else, Mom interrupted me. "So let me get this straight. Basically what you're saying is you do not have the means to protect my daughter against a hostile environment, and she would be better served at another school?"

Dr. Micheltree glanced over at Mr. Sands before she replied. "Yes, I suppose that's what we're saying."

Mom nodded. She snatched up her purse and threw it onto her shoulder. "All right then. If you're fully acknowledging you have failed my daughter, then it's time she left this school."

"Wait, Mom, no!" I cried.

She shook her head at me before turning back to Dr. Micheltree. "Please withdraw her from this shit hole you call a school, and give me the necessary paperwork to enroll her somewhere else."

I jumped off the bed and grabbed my mom's arm. "Please don't do this! I don't want to leave Newton."

"I'm not letting you stay here so you can get paralyzed or killed, Jordan."

The room began to spin around me, and I started to slide into the floor. Mr. Sands caught me and helped me back to the bed. "Jordan, you take it easy. When everything is taken care of, I'll come back to get you," Mom instructed.

I shook my head. "I just want out of here. Can't I go on to the car?"

Mom waved at me dismissively with her hand. "Whatever."

As I started to my feet, Mr. Sands brought the wheelchair over to me. "Would this help?"

I stared at it for a minute. I didn't want my last moments at Newton to be in a wheelchair. It would make me look so weak and vulnerable. All those assholes would win. I'd be slinking off into the sunset to lick my wounds.

"No, thank you, Mr. Sands. I can make it just fine."

He smiled sadly at me. "All right then, Jordan. Good luck." He held out his hand, and I shook it.

I must've had a pretty bad fall because I found myself returning his smile. "Sorry about all those times you had to call me to your office."

Mr. Sands seemed just as surprised as I was for my sudden change of heart. He cleared his throat. "That's all right. Just see that wherever you go, you make a change."

I shot him a look. "Yeah, whatever."

Slowly, I gained my footing and started to the door. The office was buzzing with kids bringing in notes and paperwork and checking out. With all the courage I could muster, I pulled my shoulders back, and I walked out of there like I was at the Miss Newton High pageant.

The moment I swept through the double doors into the sunshine, my shoulders drooped in defeat. I'd never imagined anything like this would happen. Driven from my own school. And not just driven— beaten and almost killed. I shuddered.

Mom's black Lexus was in one of the first parking spaces. I slipped inside. It smelled of her—vanilla with a hint of cigarette smoke. "Vanilla drives a man crazy, Jo-Jo," she'd always say, with a grin.

When my back hit the leather, I sucked in a painful breath. I fumbled to find the button to recline the seat. Within an instant, I was hidden from prying eyes.

It seemed like an eternity before Mom threw open her door. "Unbelievable," she groaned, as she tossed several folders in the backseat. I heard her put the key in the ignition, and then we were pealing out of the parking space. "Don't you worry, JoJo. It's all going to be okay. You don't need that school!"

My arm fell away from my eyes, and I stared over at her. "Are you shitting me?"

"No, I'm not."

"Mom, I just spent three and half years of my life at that school. Up until a few days ago, all my friends went there. Now, I'm just supposed to say, 'screw em' and go on?"

She didn't respond. Instead, she eyed the clock on the dash. It was noon. Before I knew it, she was whipping into a parking space at Longhorn's, my favorite restaurant.

"Come on."

I rolled my eyes. "Mom, in case you missed it, I was knocked unconscious like an hour ago. I need rest, not a steak."

"You're not getting a steak."

"I'm not?" I questioned.

"Well, you can. But I was thinking about a different kind of fortification."

Since it was pointless arguing with her, I merely snorted my frustration and grabbed my purse. A few seconds later at Mom's request we were sliding into a booth away from most of the lunch crowd.

The waitress came over. "And what can I get you guys?"

"I'll have a Coke," I replied, as I flipped open the menu.

I assumed Mom would order her typical water with lemon. She did, but she also added, "And I'll have an Amoretto Sour please."

When the waitress left, I arched my eyebrows at her. "Kinda early in the day for a drink, isn't it?"

"It's five o'clock somewhere," she quipped with a smile.

"Whatever, Mom."

The waitress returned with our drinks and took our order. I was about to make a comment on how nice it was to be served instead of serving someone when Mom slid the drink over to me.

"Are you kidding me?"

She shook her head. "You've had a helluva week."

"I was just hit in the head!" I countered.

Mom closed her eyes and then rubbed her temple. "And you were checked over and cleared by the school nurse. A little drink will do wonders to calm you down, Jordan."

I sighed with exasperation. "Fine." I glanced around the restaurant, making sure no one was watching, before downing the glass in two long gulps. "Happy?" I asked when Mom looked at me.

"Sure."

As the alcohol coated my stomach, I shuddered. "I remember another time you brought me to Longhorn and got me liquored up," I said, after our salads arrived.

"Oh?" Mom asked, as she drizzled a fine layer of Honey Mustard on her salad.

"Uh-huh. It was right before I went in for my abortion.

Mom gasped and dropped the small dish of dressing. It smashed onto the floor and shattered.

The waitress came hurrying over. "I'm so sorry. It just slipped right through my hands," Mom apologized.

"Oh, it's all right," the waitress, whose nametag read 'Tami", assured.

Once the mess was cleaned up, Mom turned her dark eyes toward me. "How dare you mention that today?"

"Why not? It was Carson's fault both times. I mean, he did knock me up, remember?"

Mom shook her head. "Don't do this today, Jordan. Please!"

Tami interrupted her pleas. "Can I get you another drink?"

Mom bobbed her head, and Tami headed back to the bar. "If we're strolling down memory lane, I believe he beat the shit out of you when you told him about the pregnancy, just like today," Mom said.

I flinched. "Yeah, he did. But you kept saying maybe it was for the best because it would make me have a miscarriage."

This time when Tami brought the drink, Mom grabbed it up. "Jordan, you were fifteen years old. What was I supposed to say? 'Sure sweetheart, I think it's great you're going to have a baby. Won't you look sweet at prom with a big belly? And sure I want to be a grandmother at thirty five!'"

I speared the tomato in my salad, watching the seeds and juice ooze out. "Yeah, well, maybe it was wrong of me to have an abortion, don't you ever think about that?"

Mom closed her eyes as she downed the drink. "Don't moralize to me, all right? We've both made mistakes, okay? I realize I'm not Mother of the Year, but cut me some fucking slack!"

I smeared the tomato around my salad, watching the greenery become a red, slick mess. "You said it would all work out. You said I'd get revenge," I muttered, under my breath.

"Is this what it's all about? Him?"

"Maybe."

Mom sighed. "Revenge doesn't come overnight, Jordan. It takes time to make someone suffer. You don't get something for nothing, baby girl."

I slammed my fork on the table. "So far I've gotten nothing but shit because of all of this. My car's been screwed up, everyone hates me, I've gotten death threats on the answering machine, and today," I shivered, "I was almost killed!"

Pushing her salad away, Mom then folded her hands in her lap. "So what do you want? Do you regret saying anything? Do you wish you'd just let him throw you aside like a used condom or something?"

It was then a slow pounding began in my head. "I don't know," I murmured. I brought my hand to my scalp, feeling along the bump. "I just want my life back."

I glanced up to find Mom smiling sadly at me. "You're never going to have your life back, JoJo. What we've done is done, and now whatever you had is gone."

"Thanks for the pep talk," I snapped.

She reached across the table to take my hand. "Listen to me. You just pitched a bitch fit to stay at a school that doesn't want you anymore. Baby, I could have told you it was never going to be the same."

Tears stung my eyes, and for the first time in the past few days, I regretted everything. And in that moment, I knew that if I could have taken it all back, I would have. Just to have my old life again. The life that a mere five days ago was completely different than the hell I experienced now.

"Don't cry, baby. There are good times for you still out there."

"Good things come to good people, and I sure as hell haven't been good." I wiped my eyes with the back of my sleeve and shook my head. I shook my head when Mom started to protest. "Something has to give."

She raised her eyebrows in surprise. "Oh?"

"Yeah, Mom, I'm really serious. Right now, my life could be some pathetic Lifetime movie. I'm only eighteen years old, but I've been in an abusive relationship, I've been pregnant, and not only have I had an affair with a married man, but I've accused him of rape." I snatched the napkin off the table and wiped my nose. "I mean, if this isn't the big turning point, I don't know what else is."

As the words rolled off my tongue, it sounded like someone else saying them. But deep down I knew it was the truth, and it was almost freeing to say the words out-loud. I mean, anyone could see I had totally fucked up my life, and there was no one else to blame but me. So, in the same token, there was no one else to get me outta the shithole but me.

I didn't want this darkness hanging over me anymore. I wanted peace and some semblance of a new life. I couldn't cling to the Old Jordan anymore. I had to become reborn.

Across the table, Mom remained silent. "All right, JoJo, if you're serious, you know that I support you. We can drop the charges against Coach T. We'll enroll you at this Pathways school, and you can start seeing my therapist—"

"No therapists." I'd been that route before just after my dad left. There's nothing to make you feel like a total loser than going to a "kiddie shrink".

Tami interrupted us by bringing our food. Suddenly, I didn't have much of an appetite. Mom must of noticed because she said, "Tami, would you be a dear and bring us some to-go boxes? We're going to have to be leaving soon."

"Yes, ma'am."

When she left, Mom looked at me. "You need to eat, JoJo."

Obediently like a child, I lifted the knife and cut into my steak. After three bites, I glanced up at her. "Satisfied?"

She nodded. She'd only been toying with her food anyway. "If you're not going to go to therapy, what change are you going to make?"

It was at that moment that something bizarrely divine happened. Something I could have almost blown off if it hadn't happened before my eyes. Two nuns walked in the door with their arms loaded down with packages. I'd never seen shopping nuns before, but it was all the sign I needed.

"I want to go to school at Saint Catherine's."

Mom gasped. "That all girls school?"

"Yes."

"That Catholic school?"

"*Yes!*" I continued looking at the nuns. One of them caught my eye, and she smiled. I returned her smile. Mom glanced over her shoulder. "Are you trying to tell me you want to become a nun? Because if you are, I'm taking you to the fucking hospital right now!"

I fought not to laugh in her face since her outrage was quite humorous. But I decided I'd better reassure her instead. "No, Mom, I don't want to become a nun. But I do want to change, and school is part of that. I just think the best thing for me would be to go to an all girls' school. Away from guys—including teachers."

Our to-go boxes arrived, and Mom started shoveling her food inside. "Want me to do yours?" she asked, when I still held my fork in midair.

"Aren't you going to tell me what you think?"

141

Mom responded by sliding my plate over and dumping it into the box. Then she dug in her purse for her debit card. After she slid it into the leather envelope, she finally looked up at me. She sighed. "Whatever you want to do, JoJo, I'm behind you."

I smiled. "Really?"

"Of course. For better or worse, I'm your mother. So, if you want to go to school with a bunch of chicks and nuns, then I'm all for it."

"Thanks Mom."

And for the first time all week, I actually felt good. I'd had a near death experience, and I wasn't going to waste it. I was going to change, and I was going to come clean about Coach T.

Chapter Twelve *Melanie*

It was Friday afternoon, and I had a couple of hours to kill until my game. Thinking of it brought a twinge of sadness to my heart. Not only was it the first game without Coach T, but it was also the first one without us doing our 'Grizzly Den' layover. Instead of going home before the games, we would hole up in the field house. We'd order in dinner and spend the next few hours eating, laughing, texting, and talking. Coach T loved that we did it. He said it was team building.

Now our team scattered to their own corners. Maybe as team captain I should have done something about keeping the tradition, but I just didn't have it in me.

So, for the last thirty minutes, I'd reclined on my couch, watching Coach T's protest rally that I'd TiVoed. I took in every aspect: the size of the crowd, the messages on the signs, the comments from some of the players, parents, and Coach T's attorney. Of course, I searched for Will each time. He was only shown briefly as the reporter commented that Coach T's son had also turned out to support him.

Finally, I made myself turn it off. I flipped through the channels until I landed on something to cheer me up. Just as I settled down under my cozy fleece throw, the doorbell rang. I hopped up and padded down the hall. "Who is it?" I asked.

"It's Will."

My heard thudded in my chest. With shaking hands, I undid the locks and threw open the door. "Hey," I said.

"Hey," he murmured.

We both stood there, staring at each other. Finally, I stepped forward. "Wanna come in?"

He nodded. I held the door open, letting him step inside. Once he stood in the foyer, he held back, shifting nervously on his feet. When I walked back into the living room, he followed me.

I picked up the remote to turn off the TV. "*Mansfield Park*," he said.

"What?"

He pointed to the TV. "You're watching *Mansfield Park*."

"Oh, yeah," I said, color flooding my face.

A smile tugged at his lips. "You're such a sap with your romance movies."

I didn't say anything. Instead, I motioned for him to have a seat. He moved the blanket and sat down beside me. "Mel, I came over here to tell you I'm sorry."

My eyes widened in surprise. "You are?"

He nodded. "Yes, I really am. I was so stupid and such a jerk to you."

I didn't respond. After all, what could I say? He'd been more than stupid and a jerk. He'd been a mega-sized asshole.

In my hesitation, Will reached over and grabbed my hand. "Will you forgive, Mel? I promise I'll never be so stupid ever again."

I stared down at his hand intertwined with mine. "I never thought you'd be that stupid to begin with. So how do I know you aren't just making promises you won't keep?"

"But I will! I swear to you I will!" he argued.

His eyes burned into me, but I couldn't meet his gaze. "You really hurt me. I was just doing what I had to do—what my lawyer and parents said I needed to."

"I know," he murmured, his dark head hanging in shame.

"And then you giving me that bullshit ultimatum and not speaking to me yesterday."I shook my head. "It was like I didn't even know you anymore."

Will leaned towards me. "Melanie, all I can say is how very sorry I am. I guess I just snapped when I found out there was some kinda real evidence with Jordan and how you weren't going to be able to go to the rally. It blinded me, and I'm sorry." He sighed. "I don't feel like myself anymore."

I wanted to tell him I knew how he felt. That being someone else drained me, and I'd give anything to go back to the old me. But I didn't. Instead, I squeezed his hand. "I'm sorry for what you're going through, Will. I want to be here for you. I really do."

He brought his hand to my face. Slowly, his fingertips rubbed across my cheek. "Not being with you—it's been miserable."

I closed my eyes. "It has for me, too."

"Please forgive me. I can't live without you, Mel," he murmured, before leaning over to kiss me.

I jerked away before I could stop myself. It was a gut reaction—a true aversion to anything remotely sexual.

Will stared at me with questioning eyes.

Stammering, I said, "I-I'm s-sorry. I guess I'm just

gun-shy after what happened." I'd given him yet another lie. I was getting way too good at this.

The truth was I missed his kisses. I missed the way they could make with tingle with longing and feel safe and protected all at once. I knew it was strange to feel this way about him after what happened.

I cupped his face in my hands and stared into his eyes. "I love you so much it hurts," I whispered.

"I'm sorry I hurt you. I'm so, so sorry. I never want to do anything to hurt you ever again," he said.

I accepted his apology by bringing my arms around his neck. And for the moment, we were all right.

* * *

The next night found me lounging around on the couch once again while my parents rushed around getting ready for Luke's ball game. "Suzanne, have you seen my phone?" Dad shouted upstairs.

"It's on the table by the door," I replied.

Dad laughed. "What would I do without you?"

I smiled. "Who knows."

He grabbed up the phone and slid it in his pocket. Then he looked over at me. "Are you sure you don't want to come with us to Luke's game?"

"Nah, I'm tired. I'll just support him at the next home game."

Dad smiled. "All right. Call us if you need us." He went back to the staircase. "Suzanne, we have to go!"

Mom responded by rushing down the stairs in a cloud of Tresor perfume. "Okay, okay, I'm ready," she panted, clearly out of breath. She was notorious for being late.

"Still not coming?" she asked, throwing on her coat.

"Nope, I gotta hot date with popcorn and a movie."

Mom forced a smile. I could tell she was concerned by the way I'd been acting lately. Plus, I was never one to not be doing something on Friday and Saturday nights, even after games. "Okay, well, if you're sure…"

"I am."

"Then we'll see you after nine."

I nodded. "Be careful, and tell Luke to win big!"

After finding nothing on television but reality shows, I picked up my worn copy of *Pride and Prejudice*. Just as I was being swept away by Mr. Darcy, my phone buzzed next to me. It was a text from Will.

Need to talk. Be there in five.

I quickly texted back an *ok*. I didn't have to wait long for him to knock at the back door. I let him in. "Hey babe, what's wrong?" I asked.

Will didn't answer me. He gazed around the kitchen. "Where's your mom and dad?"

"They're at Luke's game—you know the Freshman play away one tonight over in Hamilton."

"Oh yeah, I forgot."

He still stood there, swaying back and forth. "Will?" I questioned.

"Let's go to the living room."

Without a word, he stalked out of the kitchen. I followed slowly behind him. Before sinking down on the couch, Will slung off his coat and threw it angrily to the floor. I hesitated in the doorway, unsure of what to say or do. When his chest began heaving in silent sobs, I crossed the room to him. "Hey, what's wrong?" I asked, as I eased down beside him on the couch.

147

He momentarily stiffened, and I knew he was embarrassed for me to see him crying. But I drew him into my arms and held him. "It's okay," I whispered in his ear. "Please tell me what's wrong."

I held him for a few moments before he pulled away. He wiped his damp eyes on his sleeve. "Because of all this shit going on, Dad can't come to Senior Night."

I gasped in shock. With everything going on, I hadn't given Senior Night much thought. It was a celebration time where players and their parents were introduced to the fans. Mothers received roses, and then both parents led their child across the court. It was a big production—something you looked forward to.

But the enormity came crashing down on me. Of course Coach T wouldn't be allowed to come. Because of his arrest, he wasn't allowed within ten feet of a school yard. So he wouldn't be able to stand beside his son—his only child—at the last home game of Will's high school career.

"I'm so sorry," I murmured, running my hand over his back.

He sighed with exasperation. "Everything is just so fucked up now. Mom's crying all the time. Dad just mopes around the house, staring at all his trophies and coaching awards. The way people look at me in the hallway..." he shook his head angrily. "And the shit they say about you-"

"It'll die down," I argued.

"When? It's been over a week, Mel, and it's still the hottest gossip at school. Now that the newspapers leaked the fact there's physical evidence, people are really believing it about Jordan. And when the trial starts." He closed his eyes and moaned. "Jesus, what will it be like then?"

My heart ached for Will. I wished there was somewhere we could escape. Somewhere far, far away from the scandal and the issues and problems that bogged us down. Maybe a tropical island where no one knew us. An island with crystal blue water and white sandy beaches. Somewhere we could be alone together. A place to drown our troubles in each other's kisses.

Without stopping to think anymore, I brought my lips to his. At first, he didn't kiss me back, but when I wrapped my arms around his neck, his lips became eager against mine.

The past week had been a living hell, and I wanted nothing more but for an escape. But then there was also a burning need crackling within me—one that shocked and revolted me. I wanted to erase any memories I had of Coach T raping me, and there was only one way to do that.

I straddled Will's hips and pushed him back against the couch. He jerked his lips from mine. "Mel, what are you doing?"

I stared into his eyes—cloudy with combustive mix of grief and longing. "I-I want to be with you."

Will's eyebrows shot up. "Are you kidding me? *Now*?"

Warmth filled my cheeks as I ducked my head and nodded. When I finally dared to meet his gaze, he was staring at me. "Don't you want to?" I whispered.

A ragged breath escaped his chest. "Of course *I* want to. But the question is after all the shit that's gone down this week, are you sure you want to?"

The truth was I needed this to happen now more than ever before. I needed to be the normal girl who slept with her high school boyfriend, not a rape victim. More than anything, sex was *my* decision this time, and I controlled whether it happened or it didn't. No one was forcing me to do anything, and it was empowering.

I picked at the rose pattern on my throw and refused to answer him. He took my hand in his. "Mel, I want to be with you more than anything in the world, but I want to know that we're doing this for the right reasons."

My heart beat erratically in my chest. "I love you so much, Will. I just want something good to happen with all this craziness around us."

He stared at me for a moment before he finally smiled. "I love you, too," he murmured. Then he kissed me, and he didn't argue or question me anymore. I slid off his lap and then stood up from the couch, pulling him up beside me. Hand and hand we walked up the stairs.

Part of me tingled with excitement. This was it. I was finally going to be with Will. We were going to make love for the first time—after all this time.

But the voices of doubt mocked me. *What do you think you're doing? You can't give yourself to him— you've already been had! And by his father.*

I reached the landing of the stairs and squeezed my eyes shut, desperately battling the raging war in my mind. *If I'm with Will, it can erase the past. Our love is powerful enough to take the rape away.* I truly believed I could delude myself into accepting he was my first—that what happened in Coach T's office was false. Yes, once we were together, it would change.

150

Will walked on ahead of me into the bedroom. I shut and locked the door behind us. I knew we had enough time. It would be hours before my parents got back home.

He waited for me in the center of the room. I took slow steps over to him. He drew me into his arms, kissing me lightly on the lips. His kisses then trailed across my cheek.

"Don't be nervous," he murmured, as his lips grazed my ear.

"I'm not," I lied. But it was impossible not to be. I wasn't just making love with him—I was using the moment to drown out the past.

Will's lips briefly met mine before his tongue swept inside my mouth. I ran my fingers through his hair. He sat me down at the edge of the bed. I glanced up at him shyly as I pulled his shirt out of his jeans. He raised his arms as I whisked his shirt away. He brought my hand to his bare chest. "I love you with all my heart, Melanie Reeves, and one day, I'm going to marry you."

I couldn't help giggling. "I'm already going to sleep with you, Will, so don't make promises you don't intend to keep!"

He shook his head. "I really mean it. I don't care if they say we're too young and don't know what we're doing. I love you, and I want to spend the rest of my life with you."

Tears stung my eyes. "You really want to marry me?"

"If I had a ring, I'd get on one knee right now!" he assured me, with a grin.

"I'd say yes," I whispered.

He kissed me. "I'm glad to hear it." Then he eased me onto my back. The moment I felt his weight on me, I began to panic. I tore my lips from his, desperate for air. Will took it as an invitation and began kissing down my neck. I closed my eyes and tried focusing on the sensation of his hands under my shirt.

But when his hand snaked down to the button of my jeans, my throat started to close up. A prickly sensation needled its way over my body before lodging in my chest. This wasn't right. I wasn't supposed to feel this way. All the pleasure and anticipation washed away, and a stone cold reality crashed down on me.

With my eyes pinched shut, I willed the feeling to go away. I tried running my fingers through his hair again. But it didn't help. Then I brought my hands to his bare chest, but as my hand touched his skin, something flickered in my mind—slow at first like glimmering images on a pond. Then it charged full force like a train.

It wasn't Will on top of me anymore with his hands roaming over my body, seeking what I had for so long denied him. It was Coach T. I heard his voice in my ear, *"Will's just a boy. What does he know? You need a man to teach you about love...you need me to teach you!"*

And then I shattered.

"No, no, no!" I screamed. Pounding against Will's chest, I flailed and writhed out of his grasp the way I had wanted to with Coach T.

"Mel, what's wrong?" Will asked.

I didn't answer him. Instead, I slid out from under him and then raced into the bathroom. I heaved the entire contents of my stomach into the toilet. Over and over I threw up until there was nothing left in me. When I finished, I collapsed onto the floor.

Will was by my side. "Are you all right?"

My body shook and convulsed all over. He squatted down beside me. "Oh God, I'm sorry. I shouldn't have pressured you to do this. I'm sorry, Mel. I'm so freakin' sorry." He tenderly pushed my hair out of my face. That tiny, insignificant gesture sent me over the edge. I began weeping. Hard, guttural sobs that shook my body.

Will wrapped me in his arms. His voice hovered over my ear. "Is this because of what's happened with my dad?"

"Oh God, Will. I can't," I moaned.

"Yes, you can. I love you, and you can tell me anything."

"Not this!"

Will shook his head.

"It'll destroy us," I whispered.

"No, it won't. Nothing can destroy us, remember?" He grabbed my face in his hands and stared into my eyes. "I love you more than life itself. Nothing you say or do is gonna change that!"

"I was…" I gulped. Flashes of what occurred in Coach T's office flickered in my mind. "He hurt me," I whispered.

"What? Who hurt you?" Will pressed.

"What Jordan said about me…it's true."

Will's brows furrowed in confusion. "Wait, they said you were raped."

I nodded weakly.

His dark eyes widened as his mouth fell open in disbelief. He could only stare at me for a few moments. "I…But why didn't you tell me?"

"I was so ashamed that I couldn't tell anyone. I locked it away somewhere deep inside of me until we started making out…then it all came back."

Finally, it hit him. The one question he hadn't asked. But by the expression forming on his face, he already knew the answer. "Who was it?" he questioned, his voice choked off by emotion.

"It's so awful. I can't!" I cried.

Will grabbed me by the shoulders, tears pooling in his dark eyes. "Tell me!" he demanded. Before I had the chance to open my mouth, he shouted, "Say it, dammit!"

Finally, I whispered, "Your dad."

The moment the words left my lips, I regretted them. I didn't have to tell him who it was. I could've lied and said it was some stranger, a serial rapist targeting young girls. I'd lied to myself for long enough about what happened. What would it hurt to keep it in?

I wished it more than anything when Will pulled away from me. The horror in his eyes broke me. I didn't know what it meant to have a nervous breakdown. I'd heard people jokingly exaggerate that they'd had one. Until that moment on my bathroom floor, I had no concept.

Then the frayed strands of my sanity that I'd fought so hard to keep together snapped in two, and I started to free fall into chaos.

First, I screamed.

I screamed and I screamed until I was hoarse. Then my screams turned over to cries of agony. Pain, both physical and emotional, consumed me. Will tried to console me, but it was useless. He panicked and called my parents.

When they heard my sobs in the background, they told him to call the paramedics. So he did. By the time they arrived, I was spent of emotions. Instead, I lay motionless on the floor. They were a hazy blur of blue uniforms and soft voices. I could hear them calling my name from far off—like I was under the surface of water. But I couldn't muster the strength to reply. I heard crying behind me. It must've been Will because one of the paramedics said, "Don't worry, son, we're gonna take good care of her."

Then I felt myself floating upwards as they put me on a gurney. I rattled and shook as they pulled me out of the house. The flashing lights hurt my eyes. But then a needle pierced my vein, bringing liquid peace to my soul.

Chapter Thirteen *Jordan*

It was just another Friday afternoon. But in a way, it was special. It marked one week down at my new school. One week and counting of the new and improved Jordan Marie Solano.

Even though I didn't want to admit it, I liked St. Catherine's. No tension or sexual pressure hung in the air. All of that was reserved for outside of school. Within the building, it was just three hundred girls focused on their education.

It really was freeing. I went to school with no makeup and my hair pulled back in a ponytail. I mean, there was no one I had to impress—no one to dress up for, to slink around like a sex kitten for. Nope, just the nuns.

And I liked it that way.

The day Carson beat me up in the locker room, I officially swore off men. They'd caused too much trouble in my life—not to mention the fact I didn't want to follow in my mother's footsteps. Basically, I went to school, did my homework, and worked.

So far, I had no contact with anyone from the Newton world. I desperately wanted to hear from Tara, but she would never return my phone calls. I knew from the newspapers that Coach T was out on bail awaiting the trial. Dread filled me at the thoughts of to running into him again. Not that I worried about what he might do if he saw me. Instead, I worried about my reaction. It had been two weeks of slowly weaning myself off him. Two weeks of telling myself every day I no longer loved him. Two weeks of each day realizing what a fool I'd been.

Every day Mom broached the subject of going to the authorities and dropping the case. Each time she did, I said I would do it tomorrow. It was just too much to bear at the moment.

Even though little time had passed, it was like I went in one world and then woke up in another. One day I was myself and then the next I was someone entirely different. It was a little frightening—like waking up as a clone.

I breezed into Fiorenza's at a little past four. My work clothes were stowed in the duffel bag on my shoulder. As Marcus came around the corner, his eyes roved over my uniform, and then he whistled. "Damn, Jordan! Rocking the naughty school girl look, are we?"

I snorted. "You're so original, Marcus."

He laughed. "It's a good look on you."

"Whatever," I muttered, as I headed into the back storeroom to change. The revolving door swung behind me as I snuck over to one of the corners, away from the prying eyes of pervy Italian waiters.

I stripped off my navy vest and started unbuttoning my shirt. After I slid it off, I tossed it over a rack of tomato sauce. I had just started easing off my skirt when someone burst through the door. "What the—" I muttered.

His arms were loaded down with boxes. Before I could wiggle back into my skirt, he turned to face me. "Jesus," said.

It was then I got a good look at him. He had dark hair, buzzed short. The blue eyes that drank in every curve on me were the clearest I'd ever seen. In the light, I caught the gleam of piercings in his chin and ears. Even through the white shirt of Fiorenza uniform, I could see his arms inked in blue and green tattoos.

He continued to stand there, staring at me. I cocked my eyebrows at him. "Hey asshole, do you mind?"

"Oh damn, um, yeah, uh sorry. Excuse me," he said, before he spun around and promptly tripped over a mound of boxes. A great commotion ensued as they all toppled over on him. Then he gave a low moan.

Without thinking, I raced over to him. Frantically, I began pushing and shoving boxes off of him. I cleared enough to see his face and gasped. "Oh shit, you're hurt!"

A large gash ran across his forehead, sending blood oozing down his face. I turned back and ran over to my clothes. I grabbed up the white shirt and hurried back over to him.

I started to bring the shirt to his forehead, but he swatted it away. "No, it'll ruin it!"

"But we have to stop the bleeding," I said, pressing it against him. He stopped arguing with me and lay back against the floor.

That's when I realized since I was kneeling over him in nothing but my skirt and bra, he had one hell of a view. *Way to go, Jordan. Nice of you to expose yourself so soon to a guy after swearing them off!*

He must've read my thoughts. "Here I've got this. You go ahead and change."

"Okay." I went back to the corner where I was before. I snatched up my shirt and threw it on and then I grabbed the khaki pants out of the bag and slid them up with my skirt still on. It didn't make it down as easy with the pants on, and I must've have grunted and strained pretty loudly because I heard his laughter.

"I would've closed my eyes, you know," he called from across the room.

I whirled around and shot him a look. "Why bother? You'd already ogled every inch of me. What was left?"

Slowly, he rose to his feet. He wobbled a little at first before he strode over to me. "If that's the case, then why did you put your pants on first?" When I didn't say anything, he grinned. "Pity, cuz I would've enjoyed a view of your ass."

I snorted. "Wow, you're a real sweet talker, huh?"

He crossed his arms over his chest. "Yeah, actually I am. Get to know me and you'll see."

"Um, hmm, I don't think that's necessary." I eyed him up and down. "So what are you doing here anyway?"

"Manny hired me. I'm the new cook."

"Good for you." I glanced at my watch. "Well, try not to kill yourself again, okay?"

He grinned. "If I knew it'd bring an angel of mercy like you, I'd do it every day, maybe even every hour."

I rolled my eyes and started for the door. "Nice pick up lines."

"Wait," he said. I turned back around. "We haven't been introduced." He thrust out his hand. "I'm Nick DeLuca."

I gingerly took it in mine. Instantly, electricity pulsed through me. *Oh shit, not again. Do not even think about it!* I tried not focusing on how his hands were surprisingly soft for such a rough looking guy. Finally, I found my voice. "I'm Jordan Solano."

He nodded. "Nice to meet you."

We stood there staring at each other before I finally cleared my throat. "Yeah, well, I better go. Manny will be on my ass for being late."

"Okay."

Nick leaned over and picked up my bag. "I'm really sorry about your shirt. I wish you'd let me pay you."

"No, no, it's okay. My mom bought a ton of them on Monday for my new school."

He handed it to me, and I quickly tossed it in the bag. "Well, thanks again," he said, before I walked outside.

We were actually fairly busy that night, and I didn't get a break until almost eight. "Hey Jordan, take out the trash before you take your fifteen minutes," Manny instructed.

"Thanks a lot," I grumbled as I swept up the overflowing black bag of trash. The moment I opened the back door, a cloud of smoke blew into my face. Nick sat on the edge of the cement steps, a cigarette in hand.

He whirled around. "Hey, Jordan."

"Hey yourself."

"Taking a break?"

I nodded as I tossed the trash into the dumpster before walking over to him.

"Wanna sit down?" he asked.

My mind screamed, *No, I shouldn't. I should right back around and get my ass inside—where I'd be safe...away from you!* But I smiled and eased down beside him. When I did, a black case fell at his feet, causing my heart to sink.

He met my eyes, and I shook my head. "Listen, dude, that's not cool."

"Look, I can explain—"

I held up my hand. "No, there's no explaining. You're obviously out here shooting up or something with that drug case."

Suddenly, he was laughing really hysterically at my side.

I rolled my eyes. "Yeah, being high is so funny. Your shit could lose Manny his license or something."

"Jordan," he began, still unable to contain his laughter, "this isn't a drug case."

I arched my eyebrows. "It isn't?"

He shook his head. Without taking his eyes off of mine, he leaned forward and picked it up. He handed it to me.

"See for yourself."

I gingerly took it in my hands. My fingers found the zipper on the side, and I slid it open. When I saw what it was, I stared up at him in surprise. "This is a Bible."

"Yep, it sure is."

"But…" I stared dumbly at the black Bible with the gold embossed lettering.

"Hmm, I think I get what you're implying. What's a guy like me doing out here with the good book?"

I blushed, maybe for the first time in my entire life. "I'm sorry."

Nick grinned. "It's okay. I'd probably think the same thing." He stubbed his cigarette out on the concrete and looked back up at me. "Want me to tell you why?"

In the true smartass fashion of the Old Jordan, I said, "Not if you're gonna preach to me or try to save my soul or something!"

"No, I'm not going to preach to you," he assured. His grin spread across his face, causing those beautiful baby blues to twinkle.

"All right then."

Drawing in a ragged breath, he said, "I've led a pretty messed up life the past couple of years."

"I'm sorry," I murmured.

Nick shrugged. "It's okay." He glanced over at me with a serious expression. "This time last year you would've found me with a drug case. I was a junkie living on the streets. But one day, I decided I wanted to get clean. I wanted to make something of myself. So, I got help, and I've been clean ever since."

"And the Bible?" I asked.

He tapped the casing with his fingers. "It's all part of me rebuilding my life. You know, part of the Twelve Steps of AA—alcohol was just another one of my vices."

I stared in amazement at him. No one had ever been that open and vulnerable with me—especially someone I barely knew. "Why did you just tell me that?" I asked, my voice barely a whisper.

"Because I saw something in you—something that made me realize I could trust you."

I smirked at him. "I suppose seeing my boobs had nothing to do with it?"

Nick laughed. I liked how it sounded—it warmed me from my head to my toes. "No, Jordan, seeing your rack had nothing to do with it, I promise. I'm so much deeper than that."

We sat in silence. Nick lit another cigarette. I leaned over and snatched it from his fingers. I brought it to my lips and took a long drag. I handed it back to him. "Interesting," he said. "I wouldn't have pegged you for a smoker."

"We all have our dirty little habits."

Nick chuckled. "Yeah, I guess we do. I gave up two nasty habits only to embrace another."

Manny interrupted us by poking his head out the door. "You two have had a long enough break."

"Yeah, yeah," I muttered, rising to my feet. I turned back to Nick. "Thanks for the smoke."

"Anytime," he replied, with a smile.

As I reached for the door, his voice made me shudder. "Jordan, I'm here for you whenever you want to tell me your story."

Chapter Fourteen *Melanie*

Voices whispered around me in the shadowy realms of my consciousness. My eyelids fluttered as I tried to break through to where they were. Light streamed around me as I took in my surroundings.

I was in a hospital room. Across from me, my mom and dad lounged in uncomfortable straight back chairs. Luke perched on the window ledge, his legs dangling over the edge.

My mom's eyes met mine. "Melly!" At once she was by my side, clutching my hand in hers. "Oh baby, we're so glad you're awake," she said, leaning over to kiss my cheek.

Speaking seemed foreign, especially when my mouth felt like it was filled with saw dust. I cleared my throat several times. "How long have I been asleep?"

Mom didn't reply. Through the shroud of her hair, she glanced over at my dad. He stepped forward. "You've been in and out for the last few days," he replied.

I gasped. "Days?" How was it possible to be unconscious for days? Had I been in a coma? My frantic thoughts must have played out on my face because Mom leaned forward and stroked my cheek.

"The doctors thought it best to keep you medicated…in your condition."

My eyebrows arched at the mention of *condition*. "What do you mean?"

"Maybe Luke and I should go get a Coke," Dad suggested.

Mom nodded as Luke reluctantly hopped down. As he swept by my bed, he gave me a weak smile.

When the door closed behind them, Mom eased down on the bed beside me. "Melanie, the doctors have kept you medicated because you suffered a breakdown the other night."

"I did?"

My mind felt like a wasteland saturated with foggy wisps of thoughts and memories. "What caused it?" I demanded.

Mom stared down at her hands. "You admitted to…" She drew in a deep breath. "You told Will you had been raped."

Raped. The one word cut a jagged path through the fog. Everything came flooding back to me. I shuddered.

I told Will the truth. I admitted the unbelievable and unthinkable. Coach T had raped me. His *father* had raped me.

"What about Will?" I croaked. "Has he been to see me?"

Mom bit her lip. "We haven't talked to Will since the other night."

The knife tore further into me, causing searing pain to radiate through my chest. It pulsed like an artery had been severed. In truth, I wished it had. A major artery meant I could hemorrhage to death. Slow and easy…and then all this pain would be over. The hellish nightmare that was my life would be no more.

"It's going to be all right, Melanie. You are going to be all right. A doctor examined you—"

165

My gasp interrupted her. Thank God I had been unconscious when they did it. I couldn't imagine having to endure the exam.

Mom chewed her lip. "In time," she paused, "you'll be as good as new."

I stared at her in disbelief. How could she possibly sit there and say that? The coach who had pushed me to excel on the court, the man I had spent endless hours with in a place where I was always loved, had taken my innocence—in every sense, both literally and figuratively

Without a word to Mom, I pressed the nurse's button. "Yes?" a voice questioned.

"I'm in pain," I croaked.

"I'll be right there."

I could feel Mom's concern bearing down on me. So I turned away from her.

"Melanie…"

"I don't want to talk anymore. I'm tired. I just want to sleep."

Before Mom could argue any further, the nurse came through the door. A part of me clapped gleefully as she inserted the needle into my IV. Within seconds, I was floating away. From the room, all my problems, from Will, and from the nightmare that had become my life.

* **

When I woke again, it was dark. Dad sat beside my bed reading the newspaper. "Hey sleepy, you ready for some dinner?" he asked. He lifted the lid of the culinary delight provided by the hospital. I gagged as the smell hit my nose.

"I'm not hungry," I murmured.

"Want me to go get you a hamburger or some chicken tenders?"

I knew I didn't want any of it, but I also knew if I sent him on a mission, it meant I could get another shot while he was gone. I'd be out of it by the time he returned. So I nodded. "Yeah, chicken tenders sound good."

He bent over and kissed me on the forehead. "I'll be back as soon as I can."

I nodded. As soon as I heard the door click behind him, I pushed the button, summoning the liquid miracle for my problems.

Chapter Fifteen *Melanie*

I woke up in a drug induced daze. I blinked several times, trying to clear my clouded eyes. I peered around the room, searching for my parents. Instead, a doctor I'd never seen before sat in the chair beside my bed. She smiled at me. "Good morning, Melanie."

I pulled myself into a sitting position and smoothed down my wild hair. "Morning."

"It's nice to meet you. I'm Dr. Leighton," she said, offering her hand.

I warily eyed it. The Old Melanie screamed to be polite and shake it, but the New Melanie just wasn't in the mood. "Hi," I mumbled.

Dr. Leighton took her hand back and sat down in the chair beside the bed. "Melanie, I'm a therapist, and I'm here to talk to you about why you were hospitalized."

"Do you honestly think I need you to talk to me about why I was hospitalized? I'm fully aware of what happened and how my life is over. But I remained silent. Dr. Leighton continued on, "I understand that something truly horrific has happened to you. I want you know you shouldn't feel threatened or embarrassed to open up to me. I'm only here to help you."

I still refused to look at her. Instead, I stared down at the hospital bracelet circling my wrist. The last thing on earth I wanted to do was talk to a therapist. Acknowledging what had happened to me was bad enough, but the thoughts of spilling my guts of every sordid detail made my skin crawl.

Dr. Leighton cleared her throat. "I know that right now, it seems too hard to talk about. But in time, you'll see that bottling it inside isn't going to help you."

Ugh, I just wanted her to leave me alone. So I jerked my head up and glared at her. "So you want to help me, huh? You *understand* what happened to me?" I shook my head. "You don't know anything about what happened to me, and you certainly don't understand!"

Tears welled in my eyes, and I bit my lip to keep them inside. I refused to let her have my tears.

Dr. Leighton leaned forward. "Melanie, I do understand what you're feeling. When I was twelve years old, my step-father raped me. I loved him, and I trusted him. But he shattered all of that one day when I was home sick from school. I didn't tell anyone. For years, I allowed it to eat away at me, until he tried to rape my little sister. That's when I told everyone what happened. My stepfather is the reason I became a therapist, and he's the reason I understand how you feel."

Her story, coupled with the sincerity in her eyes, was too much. Sobs overtook me. I cried and screamed and thrashed in the bed. All the things I wanted to do that night when Coach T was raping me, but I didn't. All the things I'd done that night on my bathroom floor—the night of my breakdown.

I don't know how long it lasted. I came back to myself in Dr. Leighton's arms. She was tenderly stroking my hair just like my mother did. "That's good, Melanie. That's a good start," she whispered into my ear.

Pulling away, I wiped my nose on the back of my hand. "You mean spazzing like that is actually good?"

She laughed. "You weren't spazzing. You were dealing with your emotions, and that is healthy. You're starting the road to recovery."

"Sounds hard," I replied.

"I won't sugar coat it for you. It is going to be difficult. It's going to take time to build back your trust in people—men especially."

Will's face flashed before my eyes. I wondered if I had the strength to fight for him—for us. Suddenly, I was exhausted. "I'm really tired right now. Can we do this some other time?"

Dr. Leighton nodded. "I'll be back to see you in the morning. Get some rest."

"Okay," I replied.

Once she left the room, I buzzed for another shot.

* * *

I was watching *I Love Lucy* reruns when my door opened. I gasped in shock. My sister Natalie breezed through with a grin plastered on her face. "Hey, Melly!" Luke stood behind her, ducking his head.

"What are you doing home from college?" I asked.

"I drove in last night."

"Why?"

She raised her eyebrows in surprise. "Do I have to have a reason?"

I snorted. "Well, considering you're at a school two hours away, I would think you'd have a reason to come home on a Monday. I mean, don't you have class tomorrow?"

"Maybe," she said softly.

170

Luke still stood in the corner. "Where's Mom and Dad?" I asked.

Natalie didn't answer. Instead, she glanced back at Luke. "Um, they had to take care of something."

I leaned forward in the bed. "Why are you guys acting so weird?"

"We're not," Natalie argued. She bent over to dig something out of her purse. "I brought you some magazines. I thought you might be bored." She held one of them up for me. "Look, it's Channing Tatum." She waggled her eyebrows at me. "Yum."

I sighed. "Stop pretending there's nothing wrong. I want the truth dammit!"

Before I could say anything else, Luke stepped over to my bed. I gasped. "What happened to you?"

The right side of his face was completely mangled. Angry red scratches ran down his cheek that was turning yellow and purple, and one of his eyes was blood shot.

Suddenly, I remembered what he'd said to me that day in the car—how he'd vowed if anyone said any shit about me, he'd punch his lights out. "No, Luke, please tell me you didn't fight somebody."

"I'm sorry, Mel. I had too."

"But you promised me you wouldn't!"

His brown eyes darkened with anger. "You don't know what they said."

"Let me guess. Mom and Dad are at the school trying to sort this mess out, aren't they?"

He nodded.

"What's going to happen to you?"

When Luke didn't answer me, Natalie cleared her throat. "He's suspended for the week, and he can't play in next week's games."

171

I closed my eyes. Not being able to play basketball was the worst punishment anyone could have given Luke. He lived and breathed the game just like I did. But he'd risked everything to fight someone over my honor.

Once again, it was all *my* fault.

Suddenly, I was so exhausted it felt like a tremendous effort just to keep my head up. All I wanted was to sleep. I didn't want to have to deal with anymore of my problems, and I couldn't bear looking at Luke's face. "Listen, it's time for my medicine again. And it makes me sleepy, so I guess we'll have to visit later."

Natalie appeared stung. "But I just drove in to see you!"

"I'm sorry."

She didn't say anything. Instead, she grabbed her purse and dropped the magazines on my bed. "Come on Luke, we better go."

When he started to leave, I said, "Luke, I-I'm sorry."

"It's okay, Mel," he replied. His shoulders drooped in defeat as the door closed, causing my heart to ache.

Natalie breezed past me. When she got to the door, she turned around. There were tears in her eyes. "Melanie, I'm sorry about what happened. I wish I knew what to say, but I don't."

"You don't have to say anything, Nat. The fact you came to see me really means a lot."

She nodded. "You're my little sister, and I love you."

"I love you, too," I whispered.

She hesitated. "Just don't let this defeat you, okay?"

I stared at her. "What is that supposed to mean?"

"It means that you're too strong of a person to let this ruin you. You've got too much ahead of you."

"Yeah, whatever."

She sighed. "I'll be back to see you tomorrow, okay?"

I nodded. The door closed behind her, and I covered my face with my hands. I just wanted out. With trembling hands, I reached over and buzzed for the nurse.

"Yes?" asked the voice.

"I need a shot."

"All right. Your nurse will be there in a minute."

Chapter Sixteen *Jordan*

I'll be honest. Since the night I first met Nick, I thought about him way more than I should have. I started looking forward to work more and more because I knew he'd be there. And then when I started getting butterflies in my stomach whenever I was around him, I totally and completely freaked out. So much that it sent me googling 'sex addiction' and 'codependency'. I mean, how screwed up was it that I was incapable of swearing off guys? It hadn't even been a whole month since my affair with Coach T, and here I thinking about another guy.

That's when I decided Mom was right, and I needed therapy. I wanted to find out why I still couldn't man up to tell the authorities I had lied or why depended on a man so much.

Manny interrupted my thoughts by shoving a plate of linguini in front of me. "Hey! Wake up and get this to table ten."

"Yeah, yeah," I grumbled.

As I turned to head over to my station, I almost collided with Nick. "Easy Jo-Jo, where's the fire?" he asked, giving me his signature grin.

"Just the usual Manny fire," I replied.

He chuckled before heading over to the undesignated "Senior Citizen Section". He always made a point to come out of the kitchen to talk to the regulars. He was especially sweet to this one cute little old lady named Mrs. Santoriello who had sort of adopted him as a grandson.

As I waited on the tables in my station, bits and pieces of their conversation floated back to me. I almost dropped some plates of lasagna when Mrs. Santoriello asked, "Don't you have a girlfriend, Nicky?"

I held my breath as I strained to hear his response. The customers waiting on their food gave me an odd look. "Oh, sorry," I said, putting the plates down.

"Nope, no girlfriend for me."

"And why not? A handsome young man like you should have a string of admirers."

I could almost feel Nick's cheeks reddening.

"Jordan," Mrs. Santoriello called.

"Yes, ma'am?"

"Can you tell me how it's possible Nicky doesn't have a girlfriend?"

I opened my mouth, but nothing would come out. Nick ducked his head and jammed his hands in his pockets. Since I was never one for being speechless, I fought to find my voice. "I don't know, Mrs. Santoriello."

She shook her head at my response. Just as I was about to turn to go refill glasses, she clapped her hands together. "I know! Nicky, you should date Jordan!"

Now it was my turn to blush. Jeez, not only was I *never* speechless, but I most certainly never blushed— not until I'd met Nick. "Well, Jordan and I are good friends," Nick replied.

Mrs. Santoriello was undaunted. "But lots of relationships start out as friends. Take my late husband and me. We lived two houses down from each other our whole lives, and as children, we played together every afternoon. Then in high school, we were still good friends until this one Sadie Hawkins dance. I had no one to ask or go with, so I asked him." She closed her eyes, reliving the happy memories. "We had our first kiss that night—right after we both admitted how we really felt about each other."

I glanced over at Nick. He was smiling at Mrs. Santoriello. When he caught me looking at him, he winked. It was my turn to duck my head.

"That's a very sweet story," I murmured. Before she could say anything else, I hightailed it back over to my customers to see if they needed anything.

I had just grabbed up a pitcher of sweet tea when I saw Detective Pendley standing in the doorway. I skidded to a stop. Just like I'd been avoiding Mom pressing me to go to the authorities, I'd also been avoiding any contact from the detectives or my lawyer. I just wanted everything to go away and forget that I had ever cried rape against Coach T. I was ridiculous to think I could just wish it all away. I'd created too much of a shit storm for that.

I strolled as nonchalantly as I could up to Detective Pendley. "Oh, hey, how are you?"

He forced a smile. "I'm doing better now that I'm finally able to see you."

Damn, I'd been busted. "I'm sorry. With changing schools and all, things have been pretty hectic." Trying to change the subject, I asked, "Would you like a table or booth?"

"Is there any specific reason why we're no longer able to reach you on your cell or home phone?"

"Well, we had the numbers changed because of the threats I'd been receiving."

Detective Pendley arched his eyebrows. "It would have been nice of you to share your new numbers."

I glanced away from his intense stare. "Look, I'm sorry. I've just had a lot on my mind."

"I came by today to update you on the case."

"Actually, I've been meaning to talk to you as well." I tried desperately to fight the fear creeping over me.

"Melanie Reeves has been hospitalized the past week after suffering a nervous breakdown."

My hand flew to my mouth. "Oh my God, what happened?"

"She admitted to being raped by Mark Thompson."

The pitcher of tea slid from my hand and smashed onto the floor. Ignoring the mess and the looks of shock from the other customers, I said, "She finally came clean?"

Detective Pendley nodded. "Her admission changes everything. It's practically a slam dunk case now."

"Wow, that's great," I murmured.

"I just thought you'd like to know."

I didn't know what to say or do, so I bobbed my head. "Um, yeah, I'm glad you came by. I'll have my mom call your office with our new numbers."

Smirking, Detective Pendley said, "I suppose with this news you won't avoid me or McKay anymore?"

"No," I whispered. After he breezed through the doors, I exhaled noisily. Nick appeared with a mop and started cleaning up the tea. "Oh no, let me do that. It was all my fault."

"It's okay, Jordan. I got it. Just get back to your customers."

Somehow I made it through the rest of my shift. It was like I was on auto-pilot while taking orders and filling drinks. My mind couldn't think of anything but Melanie and her breakdown.

When I was almost done closing up, I went in search of Nick. I found him in his usual spot out on the steps.

"Got a smoke?"

He grinned as he dug into his pants pocket. He passed me one of his standard Marlboro Lights. "Hey moocher, last time I checked, you work just like I do."

"Nah, I'd much rather depend on the kindness of strangers for my smoking habit," I replied, bringing the cigarette to my lips.

As Nick leaned over and lit my cigarette, I couldn't help but hold my breath. Something about having him that close just sent me tingling from head to toe. And of course, that induced a guilt trip.

When he extinguished the lighter flame, he said, "Dude, anyone who can quote Tennessee Williams can bum smokes off me anytime."

I eased down on the concrete steps beside him. "You've read *A Streetcar Named Desire*?"

"Hell yeah." I guess my face must've registered some immense surprise because he snorted. "This may shock you Jordan, but I do have other talents besides being the best Italian cook in a fifty mile radius!"

I laughed. "Yeah, yeah, I know that, smartass. It's just I didn't take you for someone who was a big reader."

Nick cocked his head at me, and I winced. "Damn. I'm sorry. That so did not come out right." Staring into his blue eyes, I couldn't control the further word vomit when I said, "I mean, I'm only reading it because we have to in school." I sighed. "Jeez, you always make me say the wrong things. I get so tongue-tied around you." Oh Jesus. Did I actually just say that to him? I wished for the parking lot to open up and swallow me from the epic embarrassment.

Flicking the ashes to the ground, Nick took another drag on his cigarette. "You don't impress me as the type of girl who gets nervous around a guy."

"Trust me, I'm usually not," I protested through a cloud of smoke.

"Then why do *I* make you nervous?"

My breath hitched in my chest. "Because I've never met a guy like you before."

"Hmm, I'm not sure whether to take that as a compliment or not."

"Coming from me, you really should."

Nick leaned forward. "And just how do you see me, Jordan?"

"You're all rough around the edges and hard core, but you're much more than that. You've got such a tender side and a good heart. I mean, like the way you're around Mrs. Santoriello."

He waved his hand dismissively. "Oh whatever. She's a sweet old lady. Anyone would want to be nice and do things for her."

I shook my head. "No, they wouldn't, especially most guys." Staring down at my hands, I added, "I'm not even sure I really would."

"That's not true."

"Yeah, it is. You don't know the real me, Nick. And trust me, if you did, you wouldn't like her cause most days I don't."

Nick extinguished his cigarette on the pavement and then turned to stare into my eyes. "Jo-Jo, we've already established I was a homeless drug addict a year ago. You want more of my sad story to convince you that you're a saint? My mom left home when I

179

was eight because my dad used to beat the hell out of her. Then I guess the crazy bastard felt guilty because he started drinking more and more until he literally drank himself to death two years later. Then I pinged around to several different foster homes, two of which were pretty much the bowels of Hell."

His voice choked off, and he shook his head. "I've done horrible things to get drugs and booze—things that make me shudder just thinking about. So trust me, I'm sure there isn't anything you could say that would make me hate you."

Tears filled my eyes. Before I could stop myself, I reached over and wrapped my arms around him. "I'm so sorry, Nick," I murmured into his ear. "You shouldn't have had to go through all that."

When I pulled away, he forced a small smile to his lips. "I'm not after your pity—just your friendship."

I knew he had just unburdened himself with something really heinous, and the only way to level the playing field would be for me to share my story. I started trembling all over at the thought of finally coming clean with him. Hearing about what had happened to Melanie made me want to tell the truth now more than ever. I didn't want to be like her—to have lies drive me crazy until I broke in two. But I feared that Nick would hate me for messing up a man's life.

I stared down at the pavement. "Nick?"

"Hmm?"

"I-I want to tell you my story."

When I glanced up, he was staring intently at me. "Are you sure?"

I nodded.

"Okay," he said, as he took one of my hands in his.

180

I drew in a deep breath and let it all out. First, I told him how my dad had walked out when I was five. Then I told him about Carson beating me and the abortion I had a fifteen. Finally, I admitted my affair with Coach T and how I'd lied about being raped to punish him.

After I finished with every sordid and disgusting detail, my chest felt like it might cave in.

We sat in silence for a few minutes. I fought the mortification that I'd actually admitted what I'd done. Rocking back and forth, I glanced at Nick to survey his reaction.

"Damn," he murmured.

Oh God. He hated me. I'd told him the truth, and now he hated me just like everyone else. I sprang up from the ground. "Jordan, wait!" he cried. He grabbed me by the arm and pulled me back down beside him. When I dared myself to look at him, I found instead of the horror stricken look I imagined Nick's expression was one of understanding. "Regardless of what you're imagining in that head of yours, I don't hate you."

"You don't."

He shook his head. "I just needed a minute to process what all you told me."

"And?"

"I won't lie and say I'm not shocked because I am." He pushed a strand of hair out of my face and tucked it behind my ear. "It's hard for me to fathom the Jordan standing before me would do something so awful and so hurtful."

Tears stung my eyes. "I know," I murmured.

"But that's the old you, right?"

"Yes."

"Then we can bury the Old Nick and Old Jordan."

"I want too. I really do," I cried.

"And you will." He gave me an encouraging smile. "I am so grateful to you for opening up to me and owning your mistakes. That took a lot of courage."

"I don't feel courageous."

"No, I'm sure you feel disgusted about what you did."

I nodded.

"And that's how I feel when I think about who I used to be." He took my hand in his. "But I'm not that person anymore, Jordan, and neither are you. We were human, and we made mistakes."

I snorted. "Yeah, well, I think the affair was a little more than a mistake!"

"Maybe it was, and maybe it wasn't. I mean, it doesn't really matter the logistics of how you fuck up your life. It's what you do to change it."

I cocked my head and soaked in his wisdom. Nick was only nineteen, but sometimes he talked like he was ninety.

He surveyed my expression before he continued. "Take Maya Angelou. She was even the madam of a whorehouse, but look at what she did with her life."

"She was?"

"Yep, she sure as hell was."

"Hmm," I murmured.

"Sometimes the shit we go through does have a purpose. If we're truly honest with ourselves, we can use that purpose to change our life for the better, not the worse." He arched his eyebrows at me. "We've established the old you is dead. What's a way you can change your life?"

"The affair? But how can I possibly take that back?"

He shook his head. "No, not the actual affair. I'm talking about the accusation you made against this coach."

"Oh," I murmured.

"You can take it back, you know."

"I know. I've wanted to for so long. But…"

"You're afraid of admitting you lied."

"No, it's not that," I said, and then I told him about what had happened to Melanie. "I guess it's I'm afraid of what will happen *after* I tell the truth."

"It's okay to be afraid, Jo-Jo. But you've got to look at it this way. Do you want to live the rest of your life wondering how things would have been different if you made it right?"

There was such truth in his words. I didn't want to wake up someday ten years down the road and realize it all could have been better because of my choices. What was the old adage "the truth shall set you free?" Maybe it could.

"No, I don't," I whispered.

He reached over and squeezed my hand. "Then make it right."

I smiled at him. "You really are amazing, did you know that?"

Nick raised his eyebrows and lit another cigarette. "You think so?"

I nodded. "Yeah, I do."

He grinned. "Then that makes two of us."

Laughing, I nudged him playfully. "There you go being an egomaniac again." When I looked up at him, he grew serious.

"All joking aside, Jordan, I really appreciate what you just said. I've never had a girl tell me I was amazing."

183

"Let me guess, except in bed?"

A small smile crept on his lips. "Well, maybe." He took a long drag on the cigarette. "But I mean it. Just like you feel trapped by who you were, that's how I feel too. Girls usually never take the chance to see me like you have. And the ones that do wanna give me a chance aren't the right kind of girls."

I shook my head. "Yeah, well, in case you missed it, I'm *not* the right kinda girl."

"You will be. It's all about what you chose to do with your purpose, remember?"

Maybe he was right, and I really could turn over a new leaf. Of course, it seemed like the cards were already stacked against me. I had eighteen years of man-bashing, boozing, and narcissism engrained in me by my mother. How would it be possible I could change all that?

"Even kids from good homes go bad, Jordan."

My eyes widened. "Okay, you're starting to freak me out the way you're reading my mind."

"You're easy to read."

"Nope, I'm just *easy*."

Nick took my hand in his. "Stop doing that. I won't let you run yourself down anymore, you got that?"

The intensity of his stare made me tremble. It unfortunately also made me tingle with longing. "Okay, I'll try not to."

"Good. Glad to hear it."

I eyed my watch. "Wow, it's already after one. We better hurry up and lock up."

He nodded and put out his cigarette. "So do you have to work tomorrow night?"

My heartbeat raced in my chest. "Um, no. Do you?"

"Nope." He ducked his head, and I could tell he was nervous about something. I bit my lip to keep from smiling. Mr. Ex-Junkie turned Wise Sage wanted to ask me out but couldn't get up the courage. Finally, he lifted his head. "You wanna hang out with me tomorrow night?"

I smiled. "Yeah, that sounds good. What did you have in mind?"

"Well, we've got this really cool service going on at church—"

My mouth fell open. "You want to take me to *church*? On a Saturday night?"

He nodded. "I think you'd really like it."

I fought the urge to laugh in his face. Church and I had never mixed. Even now at Saint Catherine's I went through the motions when we had benediction. But something about Nick's face made me want to give it a try. "Okay, I'll go."

A wide grin spread across his face, and I felt my heart flutter in my chest.

Chapter Seventeen: *Melanie*

The night after talking with Dr. Leighton was the first night I fell asleep without a shot. But it wasn't a restful sleep. I wish I could say it was because I was no longer tripping on pain medicine, but it was because I dreamed of nothing but Will.

I saw his face as clearly as if he were right in front of me. His dark eyes, his wavy brown hair, the dimples in his cheeks when he smiled. And he was always smiling in the dream. We both were. It was so vivid I could feel his touch as we walked hand in hand. His smooth fingers gliding over mine, intertwining as he brought his lips to mine.

Just as we began kissing intently, I began to wake up. *No, not now*! I pinched my eyes shut, unwilling to release myself from the dream. It was still so real I could smell his cologne. "Will," I moaned.

A sound in the room caused my eyes to snap open. They darted frantically around until I saw a shadowy figure in the chair beside me. I gasped.

"Will?"

He leaned forward. In the faint bedside light, I could see tears streaming down his cheeks.

"Is it really you? Am I still dreaming?" I asked, reaching out my hand. I didn't believe it until my fingers touched his.

"No, it's me," he whispered.

I shook my head. "I've dreamed about you all night. I-I've missed you so much."

He didn't respond.

"I-I'm sorry, Will. I'm so, so sorry!" I cried.

At my apology, his head snapped up. He was at the bed in an instant, grabbing me into his arms. "Don't you dare say that! You have nothing to be sorry for!"

For the first time since being in the hospital, I felt safe. I wrapped my arms around Will's back and squeezed until I thought I couldn't breathe. When he started to pull away, I grabbed him. "No! No, please don't stop. Please, just hold me," I begged.

He nodded. Slipping off his boots, he climbed into the bed beside me and gathered me into his arms.

And then I lost it. Sobs shook my body as my tears soaked through his shirt. "Shh, don't cry, Mel. Please don't cry," he murmured in my ear.

"I thought I'd lost you," I said, my voice muffled in his neck. He hadn't shaved, and the stubble felt rough against my cheek.

"No, you'll never lose me," he replied.

I stared up into his face. "But why haven't you been to see me?"

Will refused to meet my gaze. "I was afraid you wouldn't want me."

"How could you think that? You're *everything* to me!" I protested.

Tears spilled over his cheeks. "But I was afraid that every time you looked at me, you'd think of him and what he did to you."

"No, you're wrong. I don't think that at all, Will. When you weren't here…" I shuddered. "I didn't want to live anymore."

Anger flashed in his eyes. "Don't say that, Mel. You have so much to live for besides me!" he argued. "Besides, if you took your life, then that bastard would have taken *everything* from me!"

187

Somehow I found the courage to ask the question I was dying to know. "Does he know what happened to me?" But what I really wanted to ask was if Coach T knew I'd told the truth.

Will understood what I meant. "Yes, he knows."

I closed my eyes. "What did he say?"

"Mel..."

"Please, Will, I want to know."

He drew in a ragged breath. "He called you a lying bitch. He told me you'd come on to him—that you'd told him you'd always loved him..."

My voice was barely a whisper. "What else?"

"No," he countered. "It's too awful." When I continued staring intently at him, Will sighed. "He said you begged him to be your first—that you wanted to be with a real man, not me."

Instead of Will's voice, I heard Coach T's ringing in my ear, *Will's just a boy. You need a man to teach you about love.* My hand flew to my mouth. Then I raced from the bed. I made it to the toilet just in time to throw up. Over and over I heaved. It was like a bad deja vu moment of the last time Will and I had been together.

Just like before, he was at my side. But this time was different. This was a different Will—a broken and defeated one. After I rinsed my mouth, his haunted eyes met mine in the mirror. "Why, Mel? Why did you make me tell you that?" He shook his head. "I can't be with you if I'm only going to cause you pain!"

I turned around to face him. "No, you had to tell me. There can't be anymore secrets between us."

His face paled. "There's something I need to tell you. And after I say it, you may not want to be with me anymore."

My heart shuddered to a stop in my chest. "W-What are you talking about?"

Will swayed back and forth in the doorway. His hesitation drove me to the brink of what sanity I had left. "Tell me!" I demanded.

"It happened before."

"What happened?"

Will's expression pained. "My dad and a young girl."

I stared at him in disbelief. "When?"

"When I was in middle school."

I gasped. "Did he get brought in on charges?"

"No, she never came forward."

"Well, if she never came forward, how do you know?"

Will pinched his eyes shut. "Because I caught them."

My hand involuntarily covered my mouth. "You did?"

"Yes," he croaked. He whirled out of the bathroom. I followed close behind him. He sank down on the bed and put his head in his hands. I sat down beside him and draped my arm over his shoulders.

"Will, tell me what happened."

"It was late after one of my games. Dad said he couldn't come watch me because he had a special practice for the upcoming tournaments. Instead of riding the bus back with the team, I caught a ride home with Paul. My grandfather was dying of cancer, so my mom was out of town a lot. When I unlocked the front door, I heard these noises…And then I saw him." He met my horrified gaze. "She was a senior and his star."

"Like me," I murmured.

189

Will nodded.

"Was he raping her?"

Will's face reddened. "No, from what I saw, it was—uh, it was consensual. But even so, she screamed the moment she saw me. Dad whirled around." Will shook his head. "He told me to get the fuck out of there. So I did. I ran all the way to Paul's house where I spent the night."

"The next morning when he came to pick me up, he told me it was a mistake, and it wasn't ever going to happen again. But then he said if I told, it would just be heartache for everyone and that he could lose his job and the girl would get into a lot of trouble." Will smiled bitterly. "The son of a bitch even guilt-tripped me by saying it would break my mother's heart when she was already so sad over my grandfather."

I ran my hand over his back. "And you never told?"

He stared straight ahead. "No, I never said a word." When he turned to look at me, tears welled in his eyes. "It's my fault, Mel. If I had said something, he would've been put away, and he could never have done this to you."

I shook my head. "It isn't your fault. You were just a kid, and you didn't want to hurt your father or your mother."

Will's fists tightened into balls, and he pounded his thighs over and over again. "It is all my fault! I mean, I knew all of this when Jordan accused him, but I thought she was lying. I figured they were together just like he'd been with that other girl. But you…not you. I could've done something."

I put both my hands on each side of Will's face and forced him to look at me. "Stop it. I won't let you blame yourself."

"Yeah, but I bet you're sure as hell still taking all the blame over that bastard."

My gaze dropped to the blanket. "I..I can't help it."

A growl came from low in Will's throat. "When I found out what he had done…I wanted to kill him." He choked on his sobs. "I still want to kill him. A long, slow death where he's tortured for what he did to you."

"Don't say that."

"Why not?"

I sighed. "If you killed him, it wouldn't take away what happened. It's always going to be there. And if we're going to stay together, you're going to have to accept that."

He stared into my eyes. "But how can I accept it? How can I ever be at peace with the fact my father— my flesh and blood—raped the only girl I've ever loved?"

"I don't know how." I shook my head sadly. "I don't have all the answers yet. Maybe I never will. But I'm going to try."

"You are?"

I stared down at my hands. "Yeah, there's a really nice therapist who has been around to talk to me." I peered up to meet Will's shocked eyes. "I really like her. And she's trying to help me get better," I explained.

"That's good."

"Yeah, it is."

I nervously chewed on my lip, remembering something Dr. Leighton brought up in our last session. "Will?"

"Hmm."

"If I asked you to do something, would you do it for me?"

"Of course…anything."

I drew in a deep breath before asking, "Would you come to therapy with me?"

He tensed up next to me before pulling away. "Why?"

"It would be good for you…for us."

"I don't know, Mel…I'm not one of these people who believes in feeling a bunch of shit or telling my life story to some stranger."

I nodded. "No, you're right. I shouldn't have asked."

He exhaled noisily. "Now don't do that."

"Do what?"

"Pretend that you really don't want me to do something when I know deep down you do." His lips curved into a smile. "You're a terrible liar, Mel."

"I'm sorry for lying. And you're right. I do want you to come with me, but you don't have to say anything. I just want you there for support."

"All right, I think I can handle that."

I smiled. "Thanks."

He eyed the clock on the wall. "Geez, it's after four. I guess I better be getting home."

Closing my eyes, I pressed my nose against his neck and inhaled of his comforting scent. "Why don't you stay?"

He didn't answer me. I pulled away to look in his face. "Will?"

His expression was pained. "Are you sure that's a good idea? I mean, considering the circumstances and all."

"But I like having you here with me. You make me feel safe, like I'm at home." To prove there wasn't any reason why he couldn't stay, I brought my lips to his. I pulled away and whispered, "Stay."

He answered my request by wrapping his arms tightly around me. And that night, Will and I slept together for the first time. We weren't sharing a bed after our "first time" sexual experience like I always thought we would. Instead, this time together was about different needs and desires.

Chapter Eighteen *Melanie*

Sunlight streaming through the blinds woke me.
Something heavy pressed against me. Before I could
panic, I remembered Will was with me. I peered over
to see him sleeping soundly.

I smiled to myself when I thought about the night
nurse's reaction when she walked in and saw Will in
the bed with me. She had completely freaked out and
threatened to call security. After all, my chart clearly
stated I'd been admitted for a neurotic episode
brought on by rape, and here I was in bed with some
strange guy. Luckily, I was able to assure her nothing
bad was going on, and she agreed not to throw Will
out.

It was almost time for the breakfast trays to come
around. I leaned over and kissed his neck and cheeks
until he slowly began to stir. His drowsy brown eyes
opened to meet mine. "Good morning," I said.

"Morning," he yawned. He stretched his arms over
his head. "Ow!"

"What's wrong?"

"I've gotta hell of a crick in my neck," he replied.

"Sorry."

Will stopped rubbing his neck to smile down at me.
"Don't worry about it."

"Besides the neck, did you sleep okay?" I asked.

"Actually I did." He laughed. "Did you know
you've got the cutest little snores?"

My eyes widened. "I do not!"

"Yeah, you're right. You sound more like a bear."

I laughed. "Stop teasing me," I half-heartedly commanded, running my fingers through his bed hair.

We lay there staring into each other's eyes until I finally asked, "So what happens now?"

He sighed. "I wish I knew."

I traced my finger over the stripes on his shirt. "So does everyone at school…"

"Yeah, they know it really happened," Will replied.

I jerked straight up in the bed. "Oh no," I moaned. An icy fear washed over me. How could I ever face them? How could I ever stand before the girls on my team as liar who bent the truth to save her own self?

"They understand why you lied, Mel," he said, as if he were able to read my thoughts.

"All of them do?" In truth, I wouldn't have been too surprised to have one or two who doubted my story. I mean, Coach T had been a part of our lives for four years. Most of them felt about him the same way I did…at least the way I *once* did.

Will nodded. "He was your coach. You respected him, and you didn't want to see him get into trouble."

"That's true," I murmured.

"And…"

I raised my eyebrows. "And what?"

"He was…my father."

I nodded. "Yes, he *is*."

Will's eyes darkened. "He's not my father anymore, Mel. Not after what he did to you, not after he told me the vicious things he did—just to hurt me and run you down." He shook his head. "No, he's dead to me."

I decided not to argue the point with him. I figured that was something Dr. Leighton could unearth in one of our sessions. "What about your mom?"

"She filed for divorce the day she found out about you."

"I'm sorry."

"It's not your fault. They'd already been fighting before any of this happened. I guess, they hadn't been happy for a long time. Maybe that's why he hooked up with Jordan."

When Will mentioned Jordan's name, it was the first time I'd thought of her in a long time. I guess I was too wrapped up in my own drama to consider her. "So what's happened with Jordan?"

Will shrugged. "I don't know exactly. There was this whole drama of Carson Ridings coming to school and beating her up. She withdrew from Newton, but no one really knows where she went. Somebody said they thought she was going to St. Catherine's. She's probably heard what happened to you by now."

My chest tightened. "She already knew," I replied.

"What?"

"Jordan confronted me in the bathrooms the day she came back."

Will leaned forward. "About what?" Since I didn't know how to mention the underwear, I remained silent. "Melanie?" he prompted.

Closing my eyes, I finally said, "S-She found my panties in the futon cushions in your dad's office."

A cross between a growl and a cry erupted from the back of Will's throat, but I continued on. "At first, she thought I had...that I was having an affair with him." I shook my head. "And then somehow she knew the truth."

"So that's why she initially told the investigators that you were a victim too?"

I nodded.

196

"Damn."

The rattling of the breakfast trays coming around interrupted us. When I opened the lid, I wrinkled my nose. I didn't have much of an appetite, which was good since the food tasted terrible. "Wanna help me eat this?" I asked Will.

He nodded. After we finished, Will glanced over at me. "Want me to stay until your parents get here?"

"I'd like that."

He smiled. "Then I'll stay."

Chapter Nineteen *Jordan*

On Saturday night, I stood in front of my closet debating what to wear. Nick had told me to dress casually, but I didn't know exactly how casual he meant. With time ticking by, I finally choose a simple black skirt with a purple sweater. I made sure that it wasn't one of my more cleavage baring ones. I didn't think it was right to flash my boobs in church, but at the same time, I also didn't want to show too much skin to Nick either.

Promptly at seven, Nick rang the doorbell. I slipped into my black knee boots and then ran down stairs. When I threw open the door, Nick drank in my appearance from head to toe. "You look amazing," he said.

"Thanks. So do you."

And it was the truth. The sight of him in his black dress shirt and black pants sent my heart racing. With his electric purple tie, we appeared to have color coordinated.

We stood awkwardly for a moment. "Why don't you come in while I get my coat?"

"Sure," he said, as he stepped inside the foyer. As I went to the closet, I noticed him sizing up the living room. "You have a really beautiful house."

"Thanks," I said, as I pulled on my coat. "I'd introduce you to my mom, but she's out with her boyfriend."

Nick smiled. "That's okay. Some other time." A hopeful look twinkled in his eyes.

I nodded.

"Okay, then, let's get going."

When we got outside, I slid into Nick's older model Honda. It had a comforting feeling to it, mainly because it smelled like him. As we made the drive across town, we didn't talk. Instead, we listened to the radio. I wasn't really sure what to say. I knew this wasn't supposed to be a date. We were just hanging out. I mean, he was taking me to church on a Saturday night for goodness sake. How much more undate-like could you get?

But it really felt like a date, and I wasn't sure I was ready for it. Not to mention I was supposed to be giving up men, although my new therapist didn't think the cold turkey approach was in my best interest. Personally, I didn't like the shame or guilt that coursed through me when I thought about being with Nick. I also didn't like that tiny flicker still burning within me for Coach T.

When we arrived at the church, I knew I was in for a whole new ball game when I saw what appeared to be a group of Hells Angels motorcycle guys. "Um is this Biker Heaven or something?" I asked.

Nick laughed. "No, smartass it isn't. Now will you please promise to keep an open mind during the service?"

"I'll try," I grumbled.

The "church" wasn't an actual church. Instead, it was a large room in an abandoned warehouse. The moment we walked through the door, my ears stung from the screamo music blaring out of the speakers. It took me a few seconds to realize it was *Christian*

199

screamo. Hmm, I was definitely out of St. Catherine's territory.

Nick spoke to everyone, and I could tell people were touched by him here just like they were at work. They all sized me up—I guess deciding if I was the right kind of girl for him. But those looks were fleeting, and I found more acceptance than I'd experience in a long, long time. It was really nice.

As the band struck up a few contemporary songs, Nick leaned over. "You're really going to like Henry, the pastor."

I cocked my eyebrows while fighting not to sound like a smart ass with an "I highly doubt it" response.

"He was a junkie too, but he's even more hardcore than me because he did time."

I gasped. "You mean the church's pastor is a felon?"

"Redemption, remember?"

"If you say so," I mumbled.

"He had a life altering experience in prison. Now he owns a business, lives in the suburbs and has a wife and three kids." Nick grinned at me. "Aren't you impressed?"

"Oh yeah, just shows there's hope for all us sinners."

He shook his head at me and then turned his attention back to the music. I passed the time by surveying the congregation and wondering what their back stories were like. When the pastor got up, I tried really hard to pay attention, for Nick's sake, but it was hard. My mind wanted to wander.

Half-way through the sermon, Nick reached over and took my hand in his. I stared up at him, and he smiled and winked, which cause my heart to flutter in my chest. This was bad—very, very bad. I wasn't supposed to be having these feelings again so soon. I ducked my head in shame when impure thoughts involving Nick rocketed through my mind.

When church was over, Nick tugged on my sweater sleeve. "I want to introduce you to Henry."

"Um, do I have to?"

Ignoring me, Nick grabbed my hand and then dragged me down the aisle. We stood in line while Henry and his wife shook hands with members.

At the sight of Nick, Henry's eyes lit up. "I'm so glad to see you here tonight," he said enthusiastically while pumping Nick's hand up and down.

Nick grinned. "I wouldn't have missed it for the world."

Henry then turned his attention to me. "And who is this lovely young lady?"

Wow, I don't think anyone had referred to me as a "lady" in years. I shook Henry's hand as Nick said, "This is my friend, Jordan."

Henry gave me his warmest smile. "It's so nice to have you. I sure hope you'll come back."

Jeez, nothing like being put on the spot, not to mention I hated to lie to a minister. "Um, yeah, sure, I'll try."

Fortunately, another church member was waiting after me to speak to Henry, so I was momentarily off the hook. Nick, with his hand resting on my lower back, led me up the aisle to where we had come in.

I exhaled noisily as we exited through the double doors. When I glanced over, Nick was grinning at me. He cuffed the back of my neck playfully. "Come on, Jordan. Let's get you out of church Hell and over to my place."

It turned out Nick's loft was in the same row of buildings as the church. It wasn't the greatest looking area in the world, but I was so proud for him. He'd come a long, long way in a year.

Nick took his keys from his jacket pocket and unlocked the door. After he opened it, he motioned for me to go in first. I took off my coat and glanced around the apartment.

"So, um, it's not much, but this is home sweet home," Nick said. He raked his hand over his dark, buzzed hair, and I could tell he was nervous showing it to me.

It might have been a bit run down on the outside, but the inside was so homey. It was one huge, open room. One part was divided into a kitchen and dining room and past that there was a living area with a worn sofa and chair. In the far corner was a double bed and chest of drawers. A partition divided what I imagined was the shower and toilet from the rest of the room.

I turned back to Nick and smiled. "It's great—I love it."

He cocked his eyebrows. "Really? I would've thought compared to your house, it's a real shithole."

I shook my head furiously, hating how he was running himself down. "That's my *mom's* house. This is *your* place. You did all of this yourself without anyone else's money. And for someone who is a recovering addict off the streets that's pretty freakin' amazing."

Nick contemplated my response. Then he grinned broadly. "Okay, then, let's get started on dinner."

I followed him over to the kitchen. "And what culinary delight are you preparing?"

"Well, I figured after working all the time in an Italian restaurant, we could do with a change. So, I thought chicken enchiladas would be good."

I bobbed my head appreciatively. "How did you know I loved Mexican food so much?"

"Lucky guess….and a good one considering I went ahead and made them earlier today!"

I laughed as Nick took out a casserole dish from the refrigerator. He passed it under my nose for inspection. "Hmm, those smell amazing."

He beamed as he set the dish aside to preheat the oven. "I figured we'd be pretty starved after we got in, so I thought I'd better plan ahead."

"I do like a man with a plan," I joked as I hopped up on one of the empty counters. Swinging my feet back and forth, I watched as Nick began gathering the onions, tomatoes, and chilies for fresh Pico de Gallo. "So where did you learn to cook?" I asked when he started dicing the veggies.

"It's actually in my blood. My dad's family owns an Italian restaurant up in Jersey. When he wasn't on a binge, my dad would do the cooking in the house. He taught me a lot of dishes that had been passed down in my family from when they were back in Sicily. I'm hoping to convince Manny to let me introduce them to the menu."

I rolled my eyes. "Good luck with that one."

The oven timer went off, and he slid the enchiladas inside. "Tell me about it."

"But hey, if your family was from Sicily, maybe you've got some mob connections that could put some heat on Manny."

Nick laughed. "That would be awesome, wouldn't it?"

I giggled. "It'd probably make working for him a lot easier. He is such a tool sometimes."

With a snort, Nick said, "I don't think he needs the mob. I think he just needs to get laid." The moment he realized what he said, his ducked his head. He busied himself fixing some chips and salsa for us to snack on.

To change the subject, I asked, "Do you ever hear from any of your dad's family?"

"Yeah, I actually talked with one of my uncles a few months ago. He'd been looking for me since I left the last foster home."

"That's great."

Nick nodded. "When he heard I wanted to go to culinary school, he asked me to come up to Jersey and run the family restaurant while I'm in school."

My heart sank. I couldn't believe the emotions coursing through me. Even though it was way too soon, I couldn't bear the thoughts of Nick leaving. Finally I found my voice again. "That's awesome."

"I haven't decided if I want to do it or not. It would be cool to have some family support after all these years."

"I can only imagine."

He slid the plate with the chips and salsa over to me. "Have you ever thought of looking up your dad?"

Shrugging, I took one of the chips and broke it apart. "Sometimes."

Nick came over and stood in front of me. "Are you afraid of what you might find out? Like what happened to him?"

"Maybe." At Nick's expectant gaze, I sighed. "Maybe I'm afraid that I'll find him living an amazing life with a new wife and kids. Maybe I'll find out that he still doesn't want to have anything to do with me, and that his greatest regret is me being born."

I hated myself when tears stung my eyes. When they spilled over my cheeks, Nick swept them away. "You won't ever know until you try," he whispered.

I bobbed my head. "Yeah, I know."

"You might find out he's been wrestling with contacting you just as much as you have him."

"That'd be cool."

Nick smiled. "Hang in there, Jordan. Things are going to work out for you."

His words made me cry harder. As I wiped my cheeks with the back of my hand, I sniffed, "Don't you get it? I've been a horrible person, Nick! I could've sent Coach T to jail if everyone believed me!" When another thought flashed in my mind, my emotional pain doubled me over in physical pain. "I killed my baby."

In an instant, Nick wrapped his arms around me as hard sobs wracked my body. "Hey now, I didn't mean to upset you. Don't cry," he crooned in my ear.

Through hiccupping breaths, I said, "I don't deserve good things to happen to me. I deserve to pay over and over for what I've done!"

He rubbed wide circles over my back. "No, you don't. It's called forgiveness, and you've got to try to forgive yourself." Pulling away, he cupped my face in his hands. "You've done some shitty things in your past. But it's the *past*. Don't look back anymore. Just look forward."

I stared into his deep blue eyes. "Do you really believe that?"

"There wouldn't be a reason for me to live anymore if I didn't focus on the future."

Gripping the sides of his shirt, I said, "Then thank goodness for that because I can't imagine a world without you in it."

At that moment, an acrid smell assaulted my nostrils. "Shit, the rice!" Nick cried, spinning away from me.

"I'm sorry."

He chuckled. "What are you apologizing for?"

I swiped the tears off my cheek with the back of my hand. "It's my fault you weren't watching the rice."

Nick shook his head at me. "Would you stop with the 'everything is Jordan's fault'?" He picked up the pot and dumped out the burnt contents. "See," he said, waving the box at me as he started on a new batch. "It's all good, so don't beat yourself up."

"I'll try," I murmured.

After my emotional melt-down, we didn't talk for a few minutes. Instead, we just listened to the radio Nick had turned on. While I started munching on the chips and salsa, Nick finally broke the silence. "So how did you like church?"

I swallowed hard. "Oh, um, it was...interesting."

Nick paused in stirring the rice and cocked his eyebrow at me. "You know you can tell me the truth, Jordan."

"I am," I insisted.

He bit his lip and then started spooning the rice into a bowl. He glanced up and smiled at my expression. "I'm sorry I'm being so pushy about it. It's just with my recovery and AA, my faith is the most important thing in my life."

I sighed. "I did like it, Nick. Everyone was so nice and accepting—I haven't had that in a long time."

"But?"

206

"It's all a little overwhelming. I mean, so much has happened to me in the last few weeks that it's going to take me a little time to process. I've never had faith before—if anything I had the opposite of it. I'm used to 'if you want it, you get it' kinda motto." I shook my head. "And faith isn't that. It's about believing in something not even tangible."

He took my words in and then nodded. "I understand."

I hesitated for a moment before saying, "But I'm willing to try."

His mouth gaped open. "You are?"

"Yeah, I am." I hopped down and took the plates off the counter. As I set them on the table, I said, "But you're going to have to cut me some slack sometimes, okay?"

He nodded.

I smiled. "More than anything, I have faith in you."

"Why?"

"Because of this." I reached out and touched his heart. "You've got the biggest heart of anyone I've ever met."

Nick leaned forward, his breath hovering on my cheek. His lips almost brushed against mine, but he jerked away. Not wanting to miss the moment, I leaned forward. Electricity charged through me at the feeling of his lips on mine. I fisted his shirt in my hands and jerked him against me. My tongue slid against his lips before thrusting into his mouth. I was so lost in the overwhelming sensations coursing through my body that I didn't realize Nick wasn't kissing me back.

Instead, his hands came to my waist, and he shoved me away. I bumped back into the counter. Dazed, I stared up at him. Oh God, I'd thrown myself at him, and he didn't want me. Everything had just been about friendship, and I had totally missed the mark.

"Jordan..." he started.

I shook my head furiously. "No, you don't have to say it. I get it. I'm a dirty, nasty whore who ruins men's lives when she doesn't get what she wants. How could you possibly want to be with someone like that!" Turning, I fled from the kitchen and raced for the door. I started to fling it open, but there were so many deadbolts I didn't know how to open it.

Nick's hand covered mine. "Stop. I don't want you to go."

Humiliation pricked against my skin like tiny knives. "Please just open the door."

"No, not until you hear me out." Taking my shoulders in his hands, he slowly turned me around. "You just totally misread what happened in the kitchen."

"Yeah right."

"Trust me when I say there isn't one fiber of my being that doesn't want to sleep with you."

I sucked in a breath. The dark, hungry look in his eyes assured me of everything I didn't want to believe in his words. "But no matter how much I want you, I can't."

"Why?" I murmured.

"Do you really want to risk what we have emotionally by becoming physical with each other?"

A contemptuous snort escaped my lips. "I don't know anything but having sex, Nick! I don't know what it's like to just date someone. I haven't had that since middle school. Dinner and a movie? All I know is dinner and sex, and if I actually got dinner, I was lucky."

"Then it's time you learned something new." When I started to protest, he shook his head. "You're worth wining and dining, Jordan. Don't sell yourself short."

I threw my hands up in exasperation. "But all of this," I motioned to my heart and then my brain, "I don't know what to do about what I feel for you there."

"So you do care for me?"

"Even though I'm confused as hell about everything that's gone on in the last month, deep down I know that I'm falling for you."

A hesitant smile formed at the corners of his lips. "You don't know how glad I am to hear that."

"Yeah, you really seemed like it in the kitchen," I grumbled.

"This isn't about rejecting you. It's about something much bigger." He drew in a ragged breath. "Because of what I've been through as well as well as the fact I'm in the Twelve Step Program, I'm not supposed to get involved in a relationship with anyone. You know, until I get my shit all straightened out." He cupped my face in his hands. "I want you so, so much, but baby, I want my sobriety most of all."

"That's okay. I understand."

He raised his eyebrows in surprise. "You do?"

Surprisingly, I did understand. I mean, I'd supposedly sworn off men to get my shit together—to find out who I was without them. Of course, I'd fallen off the wagon fairly easy and quickly to have feelings for Nick, but he wasn't my usual conquest. Maybe I could actually be friends with a guy…maybe even date without having sex.

I nodded. "I've never had a friendship with a guy before. I really like what we have right now." Glancing down at the worn wooden floor, I said, "It's the best thing that has happened to me in a long, long time—maybe ever."

Nick leaned over and cupped my chin. He pulled my head up to meet his gaze. "Really?"

I nodded.

"I feel the same way," he said.

"So like you said, I don't want to do anything that would complicate what we have. And sex would totally complicate it, right?"

"Sex is always complicated," he laughed.

"Well, not if you do it right," I replied, with a grin.

"Ah, true, very true." His smile never faded as he shook his head from side to side. "Damn. We really have the worst timing in the world, don't we?"

"Epically bad."

"I really want to be with you, Jordan."

"I want to be with you," I said. "So how do we do this? Be together but not really *be* together."

Nick appeared thoughtful. "I don't know. This is all unchartered territory for me."

"Trust me, it is for me, too."

"How about this: We're together as friends, but not officially together as a couple. *But* we're officially together to where we don't see or sleep with other people—I guess that's more for you since I can't do either one of those for AA." Nick cocked his head and laughed. "I don't even know if that makes sense or not."

I giggled. "It sorta does, and it sounds good to me."

"I'm glad to hear it." Motioning towards the table, he said, "Now let's eat."

Chapter Twenty *Melanie*

After two more days, Dr. Leighton discharged me from the hospital. Despite everything that had happened, I was ready to leave. I wanted the little things like sleeping in my own bed or watching movies on the couch. But more than anything, I wanted to move on and truly pick up the pieces of my shattered life.

Even though I was returning home, I wasn't going back to school—at least not for now. Dr. Leighton didn't think it was in my best interest. She requested I have a homebound teacher at least for the month of March. Her goal was to have me return to school after Spring Break.

On my first full afternoon home, I was trying to catch up on all the school work that I had missed. I was interrupted by the doorbell ringing. After struggling to uncover myself from three textbooks and my laptop, I headed to the door. I threw it open, fully expecting it to be Will. But it wasn't.

It was Lauren.

I almost didn't recognize her since she was engulfed by an overflowing basket of wildflowers. Bobbing 'Get Well Soon' and 'I Miss You' balloons floated around her face. "Hi," she said.

"Hi."

We stood in uncomfortable silence for a few seconds. Finally, I remembered my manners. "Would you like to come inside?"

"Sure." Peeking her head around the balloons, she stepped past me into the foyer. She hesitated, trying to anticipate where I might go. So, I led her into the den. Without an invitation for her, I plopped down on the couch.

"Um, where can I put these?" she asked.

"Oh, on the table is fine."

Lauren nodded and put them down. Then she sat down across from me on the love seat. The same eerie silence filled the room. Then she cleared her throat. "I, um, I'm sorry I haven't been by."

I responded by arching my eyebrows at her.

She flushed. "I meant to come by earlier."

"But you didn't."

She wrung her hands together like she always did when she was nervous. It used to drive Coach T crazy during games. Whenever we were down, Lauren would run down the court wringing her hands. He would yell, "How you gonna catch a pass with your hands like that?"

When I didn't say anything else, Lauren stood up. "Well, I guess I better go."

"Why?" I asked softly.

She stared at me in surprise. "Because you obviously don't want me here."

I shook my head. "That's not true. I do want you here." I drew in a deep breath. "I also wanted you at the hospital...but you never came."

Lauren slowly eased back down, her hands folding and unfolding over each other. "I'm sorry, Melanie. It was wrong of me not to come see you."

"Breanna and Kara came. Even half of the cheerleading squad came to rah-rah at my bedside. But not you...not my best friend."

She stared up at me with tears in her eyes. "Jesus, Mel, I'm sorry. I'm so, so sorry. I don't know why I couldn't come."

"You were afraid."

"What?" she asked.

I nodded. "You were afraid to look at me after you knew the truth."

"No, that's not true!" she protested, her hands rolling faster and faster.

Deciding to put her out of her misery, I crossed the room to sit by her side. "It's okay that you were afraid, Lauren. I would've been too." In a voice almost too low for her to hear, I said, "I'm still so damn afraid."

She shook her head miserably, letting the tears flow. "No, you wouldn't have. You would have been right there holding my hand, telling me everything was going to be all right. But not me."

"So I was right in what I said? That you didn't want to see me."

"Yes," she whispered.

"I guess I understand. I mean, every time you look at me, you're going to think about him and what he did."

"But why? Why do I have to think that?"

I shrugged. "I don't know. Why do I think it every time I look in the mirror, or every time Will touches me?"

Lauren's voice became strangled. "Why did it happen to you, Mel? Out of all of us, why you?"

That was the million dollar question I was desperate for an answer for. It was one that drove my need to seek help at Dr. Leighton's office twice a week. But I was still clueless…except for blaming myself. "I don't know," I answered honestly.

"But it's not fair! There you were saving yourself and waiting until you were in love, and that bastard took it all away from you!" She shot off the couch and started pacing the room. "I want to *kill* him, Mel! I want to kill him for what he did to you, and to Will, and to the team."

"I know. I feel that way too. I just hope he's going to be punished."

"Going to jail will never be enough. He deserves to fry."

I gave a mirthless laugh. "Don't you think it's kinda funny that I'm sitting here all calm while you're going ballistic?"

Lauren snorted. "Actually, I'm starting to think they must've given you a doggy bag of drugs at the hospital!"

My laughter slowly faded, and Lauren widened her eyes in horror. "Oh, Mel, I'm sorry. I shouldn't have joked about that. Of course, you're on medicine. Who the hell wouldn't be in your condition!"

I sighed in exasperation. "I'm not in a 'condition', Lauren. Stop acting like I'm freakin' fragile, and I'm going to fall apart any minute."

She held up her hands. "Okay, I'm sorry."

"And yes, I'm on anti-depressants. I'm not ashamed to admit it. I need them right now to try to keep unraveling."

"I'm glad they're helping," Lauren said.

We sat in an awkward silence for a minute or so before Lauren drew in a ragged breath. "I really am sorry, Mel. This is new territory for me. I've read about…rape, and I've seen it in movies and on TV.

214

But when it came down to it, I didn't know how to handle the fact if it happened to you. I was such an asshat for not coming to the hospital. Most of all, I'm sorry that I keep saying all the wrong things and being stupid. Regardless of everything, you're my best friend, and I love you."

I smiled. "You're not an asshat. And I understand. This is all new to me, too." When Lauren began wringing her hands again, I asked, "What it is?"

"Why did you lie?"

My brows knitted together in confusion. "What?"

Lauren stared down at her hands. "I mean, why did you lie about what happened? With Jordan's claim, it seemed like it would have been so much easier for you to just admit what happened." She raised her head to meet my gaze. "Was it for Will?"

"I thought so at first. Now I think it was more to save me from all the pain and embarrassment. I'm still trying to figure all that out."

"So, they have you going to therapy?"

"Yep. Twice a week—sometimes Mom and Dad come too."

Lauren let out a low whistle. "Wow, that's intense."

I couldn't help but laugh at her expression. "Yeah, it's pretty intense. But I like my therapist. She's young and hip. And she's been through something similar."

"Um, that's cool."

"Yeah, it is."

I could tell there was something else she wanted to ask. "What is it?"

She played with the edge of her skirt before she replied. "What about you and Will? I mean, are you guys okay?"

"We're fine," I answered a little too quickly.

"Really?"

"Yeah, really. He came to visit me in the hospital. We had a long talk about everything, and we're good." I decided it wasn't my place to tell Lauren about Will's vow to attend therapy or the fact that he and I were going to see Dr. Leighton together. It seemed a little premature to be in couple's therapy when we weren't even married, but I guess in some ways we were. I knew there would never be anyone else for me, and I was pretty sure Will felt the same way.

Before I could say anything else, Lauren reached over and hugged me. She held on to me for several long seconds.

"Hey now," I began, "what's up with all the mushy stuff? You hate hugging and PDA."

"True, very true," she replied, as she pulled away.

I cocked my eyebrow at hers and smiled. "Well, PDA with girls you hate…but JT, now that's another story!"

Lauren laughed. "Yep, once again, you know me too well."

"We've been best friends for too long, I guess."

"Yeah, we have." Her phone vibrated in her pocket. One glance and she smiled. "Speak of the devil," she murmured.

"You're being summoned, right?"

She nodded. "Listen Melanie, the team and I were all talking, and we sure hope you'll come to the banquet in two weeks."

A pain jabbed my heart at the mention of the annual end of season banquet. I'd completely forgotten about it. It was one thing to miss Senior Night, but I'd never missed a banquet in my life. Usually, I came home with my arms laden with trophies and plaques.

But this year would be different. There would be no Coach T keeping the parents in stitches with his remarks about the season. He wouldn't beam with pride as he called my name out to once again give me the MVP award. If I won this year, I would go down in the Newton Hall of Fame for being the only four time MVP winner in Girls Basketball. The bitter side of me choked back the thought that maybe he'd rigged it all these years. Maybe I wasn't the Most Valuable Player—instead I was the Most Valuable Piece of Ass.

Besides those thoughts, it would also be the first time I was put on display in front of everyone for something besides my ability. I wouldn't be the MVP—I'd be the girl Coach T raped. When I walked across the stage to the podium, every eye would be on me while every mind would be dreaming up their own ideas of how it had all gone down. Just the thought of it made me nauseous.

I shook my head and fought my gag reflex. "I don't know, Lauren. I'll have to check with Dr. Leighton."

"Okay, I understand. I just know we'd all like to see you there."

"Then maybe I'll be there."

Lauren smiled. "Sounds good."

I walked her to the door. "Thanks for the balloons and flowers. But most of all, thanks for coming by."

Without a word, Lauren put her arms around me. We stood like that—arms tightly around each other—for several seconds. "I love you, Mel."

"I love you, too."

I stood at the door and watched her bound down the stairs. She gave a final wave before pulling out of the driveway.

Chapter Twenty-One *Melanie*

As I breezed through the glass doors of the Newton County Sheriff's Department, I felt freer than I had in weeks. I tried not to let the voice in my mind mock me at how cliché that sounded. Just for the moment, I wanted to believe everything was going to be okay. Even in my happiness, I was filled with regret—regret that I hadn't come forward sooner, regret I had lied to my parents and to Will, and regret that I had blamed myself for someone else's actions.

Mom and Dad followed me outside into the intense February sunshine. I brought my hand to my face to shield my eyes. The heat radiated off my cheeks and body, making me feel rejuvenated.

We stood on the street corner, unsure of our next move. Dad jingled his change in his pockets. I fought the urge to smile. I was the one who just unloaded all my baggage, and Dad was the nervous one.

But there wasn't a manual for parents on how to proceed once your daughter admits to being raped and lying to the authorities. I guess they were doing the best they knew how. Fortunately for all of us, Detectives McKay and Pendley were understanding and sympathetic when I came forward with my confession. The hardest part was signing the deposition with everything that happened in gory detail. But somehow I got the strength to do it.

Dad brought me out of my thoughts. "So…"

"Yeah?" I asked.

"Wanna go get a bite to eat or something?"

I smiled. "Actually, there's something I really need to take care of."

Mom pushed my hair off my shoulder. "Are you sure it can't wait? Daddy and I will treat you to your favorite meal."

"No, that's okay."

She leaned in and hugged me. "I'm very proud of you, sweetie. It took a lot of courage to do what you just did."

I felt the sobs rising in my throat. *No, no, no.* There'd be no tears today. There'd been enough tears in the last few weeks to fill an ocean.

"Thanks, Mom." I hesitated to let go. It felt so good to be in her arms, to be accepted after all that had happened, that I didn't want the moment to end. But finally I pulled away. "I won't be too long, I promise."

"Okay. Just be careful and call us if you're going to be late."

I nodded. Dad paused before leaning in and kissing my cheek. He and Mom walked off together towards their car. I stood enjoying the sunshine for just a little while longer before I left.

After I cranked up, I turned up the radio. I sang along to old 90's tunes like *I'm Too Sexy*, feeling young, crazy, and goofy. It felt nice. Small bits of the Old Melanie were starting to creep back in. Dr. Leighton told me this would happen—at times when I least expected it even after really tough days.

The parking lot was fairly empty when I pulled into Fiorenza's. Jordan's black BMW convertible sat in the far corner of the lot, so I knew she was working. Detectives McKay and Pendley had thrown me for a loop when they told me that Jordan had come forward and admitted to lying. In a way, I had hoped she would cling to her lie to help me. I didn't to be the only victim. But then I was also really proud to hear that she had made things right.

As I made my way to the restaurant, my heart pounded in my ears. With a shaky hand, I reached for the doorknob. Part of me wanted to sprint back to my car, peal out of the parking lot, and never look back. But somehow I summoned my courage and walked through the doors.

The moment I stepped inside, the strong aroma of tomato sauce entered my nostrils. I stood in the foyer, craning my neck to find Jordan. Finally, I spotted her bringing two plates of lasagna to a table.

"How many?" the hostess asked.

"Um, I just need to talk to Jordan."

"Oh, well, she can't really talk right now. How about I put you in her station?"

I nodded, fighting what felt like a wad of sawdust in the back of my mouth.

The hostess led me over to an empty booth and handed me a menu. Jordan hadn't seen me yet. She came over with her pad and set a glass of water down in front of me. "Hi there, what can I—" At the sight of me in the booth, her lips smacked shut. Her head shook wildly, causing her dark ponytail to swish back and forth. A look of panic—one I never thought I would see from her—flashed on her face. "What are you doing here?"

"I need to talk to you."

"Um, I can't. I'm working."

When she started to spin away from the table, I grabbed her arm. "Please, just give me five minutes."

Jordan bit her lip and glanced over at a guy behind the bar. "Manny, I'm taking my break."

"That would be fabulous, but it's not time yet."

"I don't care!" she snapped. She gave me an apologetic smile. "Sorry, he's such a dick."

Manny mumbled something under his breath as Jordan flopped down, causing the booth seat to make a wheezing noise. She crossed her arms and stared expectantly at me across the table. "So what is it?"

Now that I had her attention, I didn't know if I could get anything out that I wanted to say. As she tapped her white tipped nails on the table—nails I dreamed of having but had to sacrifice for basketball—I cleared my throat. "I just came from the Sheriff's Department. I finally confessed to what happened with Coach T."

Her dark eyebrows shot up. "You did?"

I nodded.

"Wow," she murmured.

"I should have done it to start with but…"

Jordan gave me a sympathetic smile--one that I'd never really seen from her before. "I know things have been really bad for you."

"Guess that means you heard about the breakdown?"

She nodded.

Playing with the placement, I murmured, "Yeah, it was pretty rough."

Jordan's face continued to soften. "I'm really, really sorry, Melanie."

My eyebrows shot up in surprise. "What do you have to be sorry about? You may have lied about being raped by Coach T out of anger, but you were spot on when it came to what happened to me."

"Even though I thought it, I didn't want to believe it. I still don't. I didn't want to believe it for you or for me." She drummed her nails faster on the table. "But you see, I've been struggling with this guilt lately. If I hadn't been a vindictive bitch and claimed you were raped too, things would be so different for you. Like that I'm some way responsible for your breakdown."

Pushing the menu aside, I shook my head at her. "No, it couldn't have. Even though I thought I could, I would have never been able to keep it a secret. It just wasn't possible. I mean, I had only made it a week when I broke down."

"But you were doing so well. I mean, you had all the investigators fooled. Everyone believed you," Jordan protested.

"Everyone but me." That night with Will flashed in my mind, a nightmare I would never fully wake up from. I closed my eyes. "No, it was right that I had a breakdown. And it was right I went to the detectives and told them the truth."

Jordan shook her head. "I can't believe you really did that." At my expression of surprise, she said, "I mean, with Will and your reputation…you had so much to lose."

"Trust me. I know." I drew in a ragged breath. "But I had to. I had to tell the truth, or I would never fully heal." I smiled at her incredulous expression. "Sorry, I go to therapy a couple of times a week, and I guess it's made me sound like a complete tool."

She laughed. "Nah, you don't sound like a tool. I've been going myself."

"Really?"

"Don't you think I need it?"

I opened my mouth to say something when her boss came over. "Really Jordan, you need to get back to work. I'm not paying you to sit around and talk."

I leaned over and grabbed up my purse. I snatched a twenty out of my wallet and thrust it into his face. "I think I can buy a little more of her time. All right?"

He eyed the money before looking back at me. "Whatever you say." He took it from me and then shuffled away.

Jordan snickered. "Damn, I don't think I've ever seen that look on his face before." She shook her head. "I misjudged you."

"Is that right?"

"Yeah, I thought you were this mousy Golden Goddess who never did or said anything wrong." She grinned at me. "You've got balls, chick!"

I laughed. "Um, I don't know about that."

"Oh, I think so. I mean, you went to the detectives and told the truth. That took guts. Knowing what it might mean to you, your basketball career, and….to Will."

"He was the only thing on my mind…the only reason I wouldn't tell the truth at first."

"Jesus, I bet your therapist had a field day with that one." At my surprised look, she laughed. "It sounds like the kind of thing my mom spent hours and thousands of dollars trying to fix. Her dependency on men, which unfortunately seems to be in my DNA."

"I know. It just wasn't the right thing to do, but it was the only thing I could think of at the time."

"I understand. I mean, look what I did out of love."

I stared into her dark eyes. "So you did love Coach T?"

She sighed. "Yeah, sure I did. I mean, it was some kind of sick and twisted love since I ruined the man's life, right?"

"Jordan…" I began, but I stopped when she stared up at me with tears pooling in her eyes.

"Wanna know how fucked up I am? There's a part of me—a very small part—that still cares about him." She wiped away the tears and shook her head. "I gave my heart to a married man who just wanted me for sex. But even after everything, after being tossed aside, called a slut and a liar, after having my car keyed, and even having threats on my life…I still care about the bastard."

I reached across the table. Tentatively, I put my hand over hers. "You're not fucked up."

A painful cry escaped her lips. "Yes, I am.

"Then I am too. Because I still care about him—as a coach."

Her eyebrows shot up in surprise. "But how after everything he did to you?" She lowered her voice. "I mean, you were a virgin, weren't you?"

My throat closed up, and I fought to breathe. I gripped the edge of the booth as the night I promised Will to go all the way on the February break flashed before my mind. Regret radiated through my chest as the acid voice of doubt mocked me, *If you hadn't been such an idiot, Will would have been your first. Not his dad!"*

Jordan scooted out of the booth to slide in beside me. She grabbed my hand in hers. "Oh Melanie, I'm sorry. I should have never asked that."

For reasons unknown to myself, her presence beside me was calming. Disbelief flooded me when she rubbed wide circles over my back, trying to comfort me. Air rushed back into my lungs, and I gasped. *In and out, in and out, in and out*—the

225

breaths came slow and steady. When I turned to Jordan, tears streamed down her face.

"You didn't deserve this, Mel. I got what was coming to me. But not you…not you!"

The words Dr. Leighton had made me repeat over and over slipped easily from my lips, although I'm not so sure I believed them. "Neither of us deserved it. He was an adult. He knew better. He should have controlled himself."

Jordan smiled tentatively as she wiped her cheeks. "Sounds like someone's been paying attention in therapy."

I laughed. "Yeah, I should be getting gold stars before too long. Maybe you will too."

As Jordan opened her mouth to respond, a good-looking waiter strolled up to the table. His expression caused a grin to spread across her face. "Sorry that you had to cover for me," she said.

"Anytime," he replied, with a wink.

When he was gone, Jordan said, "Yeah, well, maybe on the gold stars for me."

"Who is he?" I asked.

Jordan's face flushed. "Just a friend. I've sworn off men."

I snorted. "You guys don't look at each other as 'just friends'."

The corners of her lips curved into a small smile. "He's totally not my type."

"Meaning he's our age?" I asked, with a grin.

"Hey!" she protested, wading up a napkin and tossing it at me.

I laughed. "So what is he like?"

"He's like me." At my confused look, she continued on. "He's been fucked up, but he's getting his act together."

I nodded. "He sounds like a keeper to me."

Jordan glanced around the restaurant before lowering her voice. "You wanna know the kicker?"

"Sure."

"We've only kissed."

"Wow, that's impressive."

"I've finally found someone who is interested in me for me—not for my body." She smiled. "It's a good feeling."

I returned her smile. "I'm sure it is."

"He's even got me going to church. He's going to make me gain ten pounds because he's always cooking for me. And sometimes he calls me for no reason, just to make sure I'm okay."

"That sounds like love." When she shrugged, I grabbed her hand. "It's okay to have a guy love you, Jordan."

"I know that," she snapped.

"So maybe you should let him in your heart," I said, softly.

She bit down on her lip. "Our pasts make it complicated in more ways than one. Plus, I don't know. Coach T's still there…Nick deserves more than what I would have to give him."

When I started to protest, she questioned, "So what about you and Will?"

"What do you mean?"

She sighed. "You know, after everything that's happened, are you guys going to be okay?"

"I hope so. We're just taking it day by day. And he's going to Tech next year, so he'll be close to home."

"That's good," Jordan said.

"I think so. I guess time will only tell." I nudged her with my leg. "Just like with you and Nick."

She rolled her eyes. "Okay, okay, I get the message." As I reached to take a sip of water, Jordan asked, "Speaking of time, what happens now with the investigation?"

"Well, the Detectives said it would be up to the district attorney about when we would go to trial."

"I see."

Now it was my time to nervously drum my fingers on the table. "The main reason I came here today was to make things right with you. But I always wanted to ask you something."

Jordan arched her dark eyebrows. "What is it?"

"I want you to testify at my trial."

She snorted. "I'm the last person on earth you need to testify! I'm a lying whore, remember?"

I shook my head. "No, you're not. The very fact you had an affair with Coach T shows his pattern of young girls." Staring down at my lap, I said, "You can also tell about how you found my panties and how I looked that night after practice."

Jordan didn't respond for a few seconds. "Okay, I'll do it."

My head snapped up. "You will?"

"Of course I will."

I reached over and hugged her. "This really means a lot to me."

When I pulled away, she said, "Really, it's not that big of a deal."

228

We sat there for a few moments before I asked another question weighing on my mind. "Do you ever think of coming back to Newton?"

Jordan shook her head. "No, I'm done there."

"But things could be different."

"Face it, Melanie. It'll be different for you when you go back, but not for me. They will never accept me—even it was true about you, I'm still the liar. The lying slut who started it all."

"Stop calling yourself those horrible names!"

She shrugged. "It's what they would say."

I sighed. "I just hate the thoughts of you not graduating from the school you went to all these years."

"Trust me, any rah-rah spirit I had for Newton is gone." She raked her hands through her ponytail and looked at me. "Besides, I kinda like St. Catherine's."

I gasped. "You do?"

Jordan laughed. "And why are you so shocked?"

"Well, I don't know. I guess, I'm just surprised that you enjoy being at an all girls school."

"Yeah, well, sometimes you end up liking things you never could imagine."

I smiled. "Yeah, you're right."

"I'm getting my act together…you know, going to class, making pretty good grades, staying out of trouble." She grinned. "Nick talks about me getting a degree in business or management. He wants to own his own restaurant someday, and he wants me to manage it."

"Jordan, I know it probably sounds stupid, but I'm really proud of you."

Her eyebrows shot up in surprise. "Seriously?"

I nodded. "It's like you've totally got your head on straight."

She smiled. "Wow, that's cool to hear. Thanks. I mean, something good had to come out of all this bullshit, right?"

I stared down at my hands. "I hope so—I mean, that's what I'm trying to believe."

"And at the end of the day, you gotta have something to believe in."

"Yeah, you do."

Jordan smiled. "Thanks for coming down, Melanie. This really means a lot."

"Yeah, I know. It does to me too."

She cocked her head at me. "What's gonna happen next? Me and you become bff?"

I laughed. "Stranger things have happened."

Chapter Twenty-Two *Jordan*

Two months later

Friday night found me working my usual shift at Fiorenza's. But this Friday night was special because I had the next week off for Spring Break. A whole week away from the nuns and school work was going to be Heaven.

Almost two months had passed since Melanie and I had made our peace. Having her on my side had really helped with Coach T out on bail awaiting his trial. We really leaned on each other, which was totally insane when you thought about it. I guess you could say we were even friends—something I never imagined in a million years.

After I took Table Nine's order, I headed back to the kitchen. Manny glanced up at me as he shoved some plates in the window. "Jordan, after you take out these Chicken Marsalas, you can go on break."

"Good deal, Bossman," I muttered, grabbing up the plates.

Once I'd delivered the food and fended off a drunk customer hitting on me, I headed outside to smoke. As I dug in my pocket for my cigarettes, I missed my smoking buddy. It was never the same working without Nick. Of course, not having him around was something I was going to have to get used to. A few weeks ago he'd finally agreed to accept his uncle's offer and move to Jersey. I hadn't taken the news very well. Since February, Nick and I had been spending all of our free time together as friends.

Allegedly just friends.

No kissing and no touching that wasn't purely friendly.

I had acted totally supportive when he told me about the move, but on the inside, I was dying. But what was I supposed to do? Tell him not to go? It was a no-win situation.

"Don't you know that's bad for you?" someone said out in the parking lot.

"Yeah and why don't you mind your own business, asshole!" I called back. But when I peered into the darkened night, I saw the figure striding toward me was Nick.

He was outfitted in khaki pants with a white dress shirt and navy blazer. I had never seen him so dressed up. I let out a low whistle. "Wow, you look *amazing*!"

"Thanks," he replied with a grin.

My chest tightened a little as I wondered the reason for his attire. "You must have some hot date tonight, huh?"

He responded by jerking me to him. "What are—" I began before he crushed his lips to mine. The moment was electric. I should have pushed him away, but I didn't. I mean, I probably should have argued about what this would mean to his sobriety. Not to mention that we were only supposed to be friends, and most friends didn't make out in parking lots. But I didn't fight it. I just gave into it.

Wrapping my arms around his neck, I pressed myself against him. My mind spun in a dizzying frenzy. Deep, languid strokes of his exploring tongue coupled with warm, inviting lips pressed to mine. No one had ever kissed me like Nick was kissing me. And with my considerable experience, that was saying a hell of a lot.

And then I realized why it was so different—I honestly and truthfully loved him.

When he pulled away, I had to steady my wobbly legs by bracing myself against the stair railing. My chest heaved, and I fought to catch my breath. As I glanced up at Nick, he was beaming down at me. "Um, what was that about?" I asked.

"I wasn't on a date tonight, silly. I was at an AA meeting—my celebratory sobriety meeting."

"Okay...." I murmured, still trying to recover from our intense make-out session.

"See, I made it to my one year sobriety, so by AA standards, that means I'm officially in play again on the dating scene."

I cocked my eyebrows at him. "I didn't realize you were such a player."

He laughed. "I'm not. There's only one person I care about being with, and that's you."

"Really?" I squeaked.

He bobbed his head. Staring into my eyes, he said, "I-I love you, Jordan."

"Oh wow," I murmured.

"Was it bad to say that?" Nick ask, his brows furrowing in concern.

"No, it wasn't. Neither was the kiss. It's just—"

"Too soon?"

"More like bad timing strikes again, don't you think? I mean, you're about to move to Jersey permanently in two weeks, so it's not the greatest time to be professing our love. I can't make relationships work under normal circumstances, so I'm pretty sure that I'd suck ass at a long distance ones!"

Nick reached into his coat pocket and took out an envelope. He grabbed one of my hands and placed the envelope in it. My eyebrows arched in surprise. "A gift for me? But tonight is your celebratory night. I have should have something for you," I protested with a smile.

Nick returned my smile. "No, tonight is about *us*."

I felt like a kid on Christmas morning as I tore into the envelope. Inside was a plane ticket. "What's this?"

"I want you to come with me to Jersey."

My heartbeat accelerated in my chest. "To meet your family and all?"

Nick nodded. "Yeah, but more to decide if it's somewhere you could live."

I gasped. "What are you saying?"

"I'm saying I want you to think about moving to Jersey with me. Rutgers University isn't far from my uncle's place. They've got a great Business and Finance program." Before I could protest, he rushed on. "I know that it seems too fast since we've only known each other for a few months, but I've gotten to know you and care for you more than anyone I've ever known."

"Me too," I murmured.

"And you've said yourself that you wanted to get the hell out of this town when you graduated."

"I know I did."

"My uncle is giving me his finished basement rent free. You wouldn't have to worry about working. I'd take care of us so you could concentrate on school."

Tears stung my eyes. Oh God, he really did want me and love me with all my baggage. He saw a future for us—no guy had ever wanted that from me before. "It sounds wonderful."

Nick's brows furrowed. "Then what's the problem?"

I forced a laugh. "That's just it. There isn't a problem. Everything sounds perfect." As I stared into his hopeful eyes, I shook my head. "It's just that being with you these past few months has been so amazing that I'm just waiting for the bad shit to catch up with me—with us."

"Jordan, how many times do I have to tell you that our pasts don't define who we are?"

"I want to believe that. I really do."

Nick pulled me into his arms. His breath hovered over my ear. "Just because we both did some bad shit and made some pretty bad mistakes doesn't mean the rest of our lives are doomed to heartache and tragedy. Sure, there will be bad things that happen, but there's gonna be good things too."

Deep down I knew Nick was right. I mean, so far I'd tried to right all the wrongs of my affair with Coach T. I'd admitted to the police I'd lied, and I'd even apologized to Dr. Micheltree and Mr. Sands. Of course, with the truth about Melanie's rape, my lies didn't seem to matter that much anymore. But they still haunted me. Maybe they always would. And maybe I would never be able to put the ghosts of the past behind me until I truly moved away and moved on.

I smiled tentatively up at him. "So, if I do come to Jersey with you, I have a few conditions."

Nick's expression brightened. "Okay, what are they?"

"First, I would live in the dorms at Rutgers or whatever college I decide on. We need to keep moving slow—*I* need to keep moving slow. I don't want us rushing into something we're not completely ready for just because of distance. I think we need space if we're going to successfully turn this friendship into something more."

He nodded. "That sounds doable."

"And second, I'd want to pay my own way and get a job. All my life I've been given everything I wanted by my mom. I don't want her or you to take care of me."

"Well, I could at least help by pulling a few strings and getting you a job at the restaurant," Nick replied.

Shaking my head, I said, "But if you're managing the restaurant for your uncle, then you'd be my boss. If I'm truly turning over a new leaf, I can't be sleeping with the boss, now can I?"

Nick jolted back. I couldn't help laughing at his expression. I cocked my head at him. "After that kiss you laid on me earlier, you can't possibly be too shocked at the thought of us *finally* having sex sometime soon."

He snorted. "Trust me, it's more a shock of me being your boss than us finally getting it on."

"Whatever, you know you were thinking about it," I laughed.

Nick's expression became much more serious. "I'll wait to be with you for as long as you need."

My mouth fell open in disbelief. "You really mean that?"

He nodded as he took my hand in his. "And then when you're ready, we won't have sex or hook-up. I'll make love to you."

His words sent a shiver of longing down my spine. I fought the urge to reach out and pinch him just to see if he was real. Surely I had to be dreaming if there was a guy standing before me who wanted me for me—the real me with all the ugliness beneath the surface—and not for my body. A guy who wanted to make love to me…that was an amazing thought.

"Jordan, your break was over five minutes ago!" Manny shouted from the doorway.

I grimaced. "The evil Boss-Man beckons."

Nick laughed. "Hmm, wonder if you'll call me that behind my back when you're working for me?"

"We'll just have to see about that," I replied, before leaning over and kissing him.

Chapter Twenty-Three *Melanie*

After my confession, the weeks sped by until suddenly it was spring. And for the first time in my life, I truly appreciate all the vibrant colors of the season. Everything meant more to me now—now that I'd been to the dark side and back. I was still racking up gold stars in therapy. So much so, that Dr. Leighton agreed to let me start back to school two weeks early.

I was excited, but at the same time, scared to death. I didn't know how people would receive me. Would I get stared at all the time in the hallway? Would people treat me like a disease? And what if there were people who didn't believe me?

But the Saturday before I was to start back on Monday, Garrison called the house. Mom and Dad were out working in the yard, so I took the call. "Melanie, I have some good news and bad news."

"Oh?"

"Yes. Mark Thompson has taken a plea deal by the prosecution and confessed to raping you."

The phone slipped through my hands and clattered noisily to the kitchen floor. My lungs constricted, and I couldn't breathe. From far off, I heard Garrison calling my name. Finally, I bent over and grabbed up the phone. In a strangled voice, I asked, "He really admitted it?"

"Yes, he did."

I exhaled with a wheeze like a deflated tire. "Well, that's good right? I mean, now I won't have to testify or Jordan."

"Right. There won't be a trial now."

"So what's the bad news?"

"By taking the deal, he gets five years tops, probably only three served."

A lump formed in my throat. "That's all?"

"I'm sorry, Melanie, but that's it. But at least it goes on the record as an admission of his guilt. Not to mention his teaching license has been revoked. He'll never teach or coach again."

I didn't know how to feel. Part of me felt vindicated that he'd owned up to what he'd done, but the other part of me was desperate to see him rot away for years in jail. And then there was the fear of running into him after he got out. I shuddered at the thought.

The next week I saw Dr. Leighton every day. Starting back to school and Coach T's plea bargain had me reeling emotionally. I barely slept at night. I worried I was having a huge set back, but Dr. Leighton assured me it was just a bump in the road. But there was also something else—something much more positive that I needed to talk about with her.

Will and I were going away together to Hilton Head, South Carolina for Spring Break. Instead of Panama City, Florida or any of the other drunken party spots, we wanted somewhere quiet where we could be alone together. He made all the arrangements for us. And while we were going to tan and take it easy, there was something else we were going to tackle.

And that was sex.

We'd been together every day since I was released from the hospital, but our relationship was totally platonic except for kissing. There was a small part of me that wanted to keep it that way. But I also knew I wanted to be with him. And even though it was evident that each of us wanted more, we were afraid of what it might to do me. But I was willing to try anything to ensure what happened with Coach T wouldn't destroy our future.

Friday afternoon before we left, I met one last time with Dr. Leighton. We talked about school and homework and graduation, and then we got around to Spring Break.

"And what are you telling your parents?" Dr. Leighton asked, a look of amusement on her face.

I blushed. "They think I'm going to the beach with Lauren and some girls from the team and that Will is going to be there with his friends."

"Ah, I see."

I ducked my head, staring at my newly painted toenails. "Is it wrong I'm lying to them? I mean, I worry about lying more than I ever have before. Even if it's the tiniest thing, I lay awake at night going over and over it."

"That's understandable considering the circumstances. Just like with your trust, it's going to take some time for you to be comfortable with what you lied about in the past."

I grinned. "Hmm, sounds like you're advocating me lying."

"Not exactly. But we're all human and all humans lie."

"Do they all lie to their parents so they can sneak off with their boyfriend?"

"Well, you're not exactly lying, are you? I mean, you will be at the beach."

I shook my head. "Dr. Leighton, I'm ashamed!"

She laughed. The timer went off, signaling our time was up. When I rose from the couch, she handed me a slip of paper. "What's this?" I asked.

"It's my cell phone. In case you need me while you're gone."

I smiled. "Dial-A-Doctor."

She nodded. "Yep, day or night."

"Thanks, I appreciate it."

Before I headed out the door, she hugged me. "Have a wonderful time, Melanie. You deserve it."

"I'll try. And thanks."

* * *

Will was waiting for me outside. We were driving my car, so his mom had dropped him off.

"All packed?" he asked.

"Yep and ready to go."

He nodded and headed around to the trunk to load his bags. When he popped it, he shot me a look. "We're only going to be gone for five days, Mel. By the looks of this, you'd think we were leaving for college!"

"Oh just quit your whining, and load the car."

He tossed his one bag in among my three and shook his head. "Women."

I swept my hands to my hips. "And what if I need all that to be beautiful for you?"

"Mel, no one is that ugly!" he said, with a grin.

I laughed. "Whatever."

During the drive, we talked and sang along to the radio. I dozed off after awhile, and Will woke me up when we arrived. We grabbed a quick bite before heading back to the condo.

The first night we were so exhausted from the drive we fell asleep as soon as our heads hit the pillow. The next day we woke up early and spent the day lounging around the beach and walking on the shore.

Just as it was getting dark, Will mumbled something about grabbing a quick shower before he headed back to the condo. I hung around on the beach, wanting to finish my book. When I walked through the door, I gasped. There was a trail of rose petals leading to the bedroom. I followed them, my feet sliding along their silky texture. Inside the room, candles flickered. I heard Will behind me, and I turned around. "This is beautiful," I murmured.

He smiled. "I wanted something beautiful for you...for us."

I wrapped my arms around him and brought my lips to his. The warmth of his tongue slid into my mouth as I ran my fingers through the silky strands of his dark hair. He held me tight in his strong embrace as all of our longing poured out in deep kisses. We moved toward the bed, each helping the other take off bits and pieces of clothing. Stripped down to our underwear, we lay back on the bed.

Staring into my eyes, Will once again brought his lips to mine as his hand tentatively came up to cup my breast. When I didn't recoil away from him or freak out, he caressed me tenderly over my bra. I wanted the feel of his hands on my bare skin, so I reached up to pull down the straps. His mouth left mine to kiss a moist trail down my neck while he palmed my naked breasts.

Desire began to pool below my waist as I took one of Will's hands and brought it between my legs. A warm, dizzying rush flooded me as he stroked and teased me. This was familiar—we had been here before many, many times over our relationship. Will knew just the right buttons to push to get me off, just as I did him. I was moving close to go over the edge when Will shifted his weight on top of me.

Then like flipping a switch, all the old memories came charging back. I huffed breaths of panic, rather than pleasure as I jerked away from him. This time instead of screaming and flailing around, I simply started crying.

Will eased up on his knees and stared down at me. "Mel, was I hurting you? I can go slower…softer."

"I can't. I just can't. I'm so sorry," I sobbed.

"Shh, don't cry. We knew this might happen," he said. He tried pulling me into his arms, but I slid out of the bed.

I couldn't stay there in that beautiful room so full of romance. I jerked up the straps of bra before sliding on my beach cover up. "Where are you going?" Will asked.

"To the beach."

"But it's dark out."

"I'll be all right," I said. Without another word to him, I slid on my flip-flops, grabbed a flashlight, and headed out the door.

I hurried across the boardwalk. My steps echoed in the silence surrounding me. When I got to the end, I slipped my shoes off and felt the cool sand between my toes. The wind had picked up. It whipped my hair against my face, making me wish I'd pulled it back into a ponytail. I walked to the edge of the shore and into the water. The waves rushed with a new urgency, and I didn't miss the subtle irony that a storm must be brewing on the horizon.

I stood in the water up to my knees, letting the waves crash against me. My tears dripped off my cheeks and fell back into the water.

"Mel?"

"I'm here," I said.

Will stepped over to me. "I got worried about you." He had a flashlight and blanket in his arms.

"I'm sorry."

He glanced around. "You should be out here by yourself. What if someone…" he trailed off. Even in the pitch blackness, I knew he was blushing.

"I'm sorry, but I just couldn't stay in that room. Everything was so perfect, and I ruined it."

"You didn't ruin it."

"Yes, I did. You tried so hard to make it beautiful for me, and I couldn't."

His pulled me into his arms and wrapped the blanket around me. "It's okay, Mel. We don't have to have sex tonight or the next night or even this week. I love you, and I'm not going anywhere."

My only response was to tremble uncontrollably. He sighed. "Come on, let's get you inside," he said.

We started back through the sand. "Can't we sit out here for awhile? It's so peaceful," I suggested.

"Whatever you want."

He took blanket off my arms and spread it on the sand. He sat down first and pulled me back in his arms. When I turned towards him, I pressed my head against his chest. A gentle *thump, thump, thump, thump* filled my ears. And I remembered; it was my favorite position.

I brought my lips to Will's. He was cautious and barely kissed me back. But when I raked my hand through his hair and pressed my tongue against his lips, he moaned.

With absolute certainty, I gently pushed him onto his back. I whisked the beach cover-up over my head. Trembling fingers found their way to my bra straps as I slowly pulled them down over my shoulders. The sound of my bra clasp snapping open caused Will to groan. "Mel, don't you know what you're doing to me?" he asked, his voice hoarse.

"Am I making you want me?" I asked.

"Yes, oh God, yes."

I smiled. "Good, cause I want you, too."

He rose up on his elbows. "Out here?"

Umm, hmm."

"Even after what happened tonight?"

"Umm, hmm."

When I brought my hands to his shorts, he fell back against the blanket. He didn't question me anymore. Instead, he gave in, and so did I.

* * *

We stayed out on the beach all night. I wanted to conquer another first—seeing the sun rise over the ocean. I felt it would be the perfect end to such a wonderful night.

And it had been wonderful…several times.

But the voice of doubt that still mocked me from time to time was afraid the sun might be blotted out by the clouds. Then the perfect image of a beach sunrise would be ruined. Then the storms would blow in. I figured Will and I would be stuck inside the rest of the day, but that wouldn't be such a bad thing.

As the streaks came across the sky, it wasn't as brilliant as it could've been. But it at least it was there—consistent and true. It made me think of mine

245

and Will's love. There would always be dark clouds that hung over us—threatening to block out our love. But no matter what happened, our love would still be there—trying to shine through whatever dark times came.

Epilogue: **WILL**
Nine Months Later

Sweat cascaded down the sides of my cheeks as I sprinted up and down the gym floor of the Georgia Tech Coliseum. Pressing on, I fought the fatigue washing over me as well as the muscles that screamed in agony. I'd been busting my ass for the last half-hour, trying to prove I deserved some playtime in tomorrow's game. Playing basketball for Tech was a dream come true—I just hadn't imagined the hard transition that going from somewhat of a senior superstar in high school to just another player in college would be. The shriek of a loud whistle brought my torture and our Friday afternoon practice to a halt. "Okay, boys. See you back tomorrow for the game," our coach shouted.

"Nice hustling, Thompson," my buddy, Jared, said as we made our way into the locker-room.

I grinned. "Thanks man. You weren't so bad yourself out there."

"Got to stick it to the douchetard seniors, right?" he asked, his dark eyes twinkling.

"Tell me about it."

Before I headed to the showers, I grabbed my clothes out of my locker. Glancing at my phone, I saw I had a text from Melanie. *Meet you at the car in fifteen. Xxoo.* I couldn't help the goofy grin from spreading across my lips. Everything about that girl was magic to me—even her cutesy little hugs and kisses on texts. It all meant so much more to me since we had been to hell and back, but somehow we had miraculously survived it together.

To say that the last part of the year was hell was a total understatement. Dealing with the fall-out from my father's arrest, and Melanie's admission of rape and her breakdown had taken its toll in more ways than one. Even though I seemed like I was dealing with everything, I was a mess. Like Mel, I hid a lot of the pain I was going through to protect those that I loved. I felt that I needed to be the man and be strong for my mom and for Melanie.

At first, there had been night terrors that left me drenched in sweat and panting to catch my breath. The dreams were always the same—I could see Melanie in my dad's office, hear her screaming for me to help her, but I couldn't get to her. I would bang on the door or punch out the glass with my fists, but it wouldn't help. It was after weeks of these horrible dreams that my mom experienced one first hand. She then demanded I see a therapist, so I agreed to see Dr. Leighton with Melanie as well as submitting to family counseling with my mom.

By the time Melanie and I started to college, things were better for us both. I was more thankful than ever that I had taken Tech's scholarship offer rather than going to Duke. Melanie and I both needed to be at the same school. Some people might've thought our dependency on each other wasn't healthy, but they didn't know what it was like to go through what we did. The tragic aspect of our past would always bond us together, but it was the strong love we had that meant the most.

Shaking myself out of my thoughts, I finished in the shower and quickly toweled dry my hair. I threw on a pair of worn jeans along sweatshirt before sending a *B right there, Baby* text to Melanie.

I was packing up my bag when my teammate Kyle asked, "Hey Thompson, wanna grab something from the Varsity with us?"

Even though the thought of running down the street to our favorite restaurant and Atlanta institution was tempting, I shook my head and tossed my practice jersey in the team clothes hamper. "Nah, man, I gotta get back home."

Glancing over my shoulder, I saw the wicked gleam flashing in Jared's eyes. "Melanie's fine ass is beckoning you, huh? Mmm, not just her fine ass. She's got an amazing pair of—"

I whirled around and jabbed a finger into his chest. "Watch it."

He gave me an exasperated snort before draping a sweat-slickened arm across my shoulder. "Come on, Big Willy. You know I'm not jonsing for your girl. Even if she's hot as hell with those long ass legs, every dude on the team knows you guys are practically married."

"Exactly," I growled.

He grinned. "Besides that fact, she ain't got eyes for anyone but your ugly mug."

Jared's words sent pulsing warmth through my chest. It wasn't just the possessive side of me that enjoyed hearing how much Melanie loved me. It's the fact that after everything we'd been through, there was no one else on earth she wanted to be with but me. And thank God that in spite of all the reasons why she shouldn't love me or want me, she still did. Endlessly.

Kyle eyed his reflection in the mirror. "Yeah, it's not just the way she looks at him. There's also that fatass rock of an engagement ring she wears when she's not on the court."

I grinned as I thought back to a month ago at Christmas when I had slipped the ring on Melanie's finger. I'd told her I'd wanted to marry her right before her breakdown. I meant it then, and I still meant it now—maybe even more than ever before. It wasn't exactly the rock like Kyle claimed or the one that I wanted it to be. Even though my mom had offered to hock her two carat ring from my dad for me to buy Melanie's, I refused. It would have just tarnished and tainted it to have anything associated with my dad—even the money from his ring. Instead, I'd sold some baseballs cards that my grandfather had left me. Someday I hoped to get her a bigger one, even though Melanie told me over and over again it was the most beautiful thing she had ever seen, and she adored it.

I slung Jared's arm off me and cocked my head at him. "Yeah, that's the truth. I just wanna make sure none of you douchebags forget it."

He snorted before slamming his locker shut. "Trust me, we won't."

I grabbed my bag and threw it over my shoulder before following Jared and Kyle out the door. After we breezed out of the gym, I said, "You guys behave tonight. You better not be dragging in your hung-over asses for the game tomorrow!"

"Shit, don't we always behave?" Jared asked with a smirk.

"Whatever. See you later." I watched as they headed down the sidewalk towards the Varsity. The last thing I wanted to do was tell Jared and Kyle the real reason why I had to get back home. Their perverted minds might've thought it was to have sex with Melanie, but they couldn't have been farther from the truth. I had a hot date, but it was with my therapist.

As I strode across the parking lot to my Jeep, I saw Melanie leaned against the bumper, her fingers furiously working over the keypad of her phone. My breath hitched a little at the sight of her in a short grey skirt, black knee boots, and a body hugging sweater. She always liked to look her best for therapy while I could have given a shit less about my jeans and Georgia Tech Yellow Jacket sweatshirt.

"Hey baby," I said.

She jerked her head up to look at me. A bright smile flashed on her face. "Hey yourself."

I pulled her into my arms to plant a lingering kiss on her lips. For so many months, we'd fought all forms of intimacy that it was so nice when she no longer tensed when I touched her. As her tongue teased along mine, I thought about the hurdles we had overcome in the sex department. Once we were finally together that night on the beach, I thought every time would be easy, but I was wrong. Some days she was ready to pounce on me, and others her emotional and physical resistance led to some serious blue balls situations for me.

I always tried to be understanding and reassure her that it was okay. Sure, I was a horny guy who had needs, but I loved Mel too much to ever pressure her or give her shit about it. As hard as it was for both of us to admit, she was a rape survivor—that was always going to make sex difficult. But I would fight the rest

251

of my life to make her feel loved, desired, and…normal both in and out of the bedroom.

"Ready to go see Dr. Feelgood?" I asked.

Mel quirked her blonde brows at me while sweeping a hand to her hip. "After all this time, do you really still have to call her that?"

I shrugged as I opened the truck door and climbed inside. Me making fun of therapy was what Dr. Leighton would call a 'coping mechanism'--a way for me to save face and still feel masculine. It wasn't easy being nineteen and in therapy because my soulless asshole of a father raped my girlfriend and was now a convicted felon rotting away in one of the state prisons I had no desire to know where he was because my resolve was still just as firm on the fact that he was dead to me. Dr. Leighton continued to have a field day with that one.

"Will, you don't have to come to therapy with me if you won't want to," Mel said, staring down at her boots rather than at me. She gladly made the thirty minute pilgrimage back home twice a week to meet with Dr. Leighton while I just joined her at one of the sessions. There was also the every other week sessions I did with my mom. I was practically a therapy junkie.

As I cranked up the Jeep, I glanced over at her. "I was just teasing you. You know that, right?"

"I hope so," she replied in a small voice.

"You know I would do anything for you." I leaned over and planted a tender kiss on her lips. "Besides, we both know this isn't just for you. I need it as well."

She ran rubbed her hand across my cheek. "Thank you."

"For what? Being your therapy buddy?"

She grinned. "No, silly. For being you."

"You're welcome," I replied with a wink. I then turned my attention back to the task of getting out of the city. As we zipped along 75 North, my cell phone rang. Glancing at the ID, I saw it was my mom. "Hey, what's up?"

"Hi sweetheart. I just wanted to let you know that I'll probably be out late if you came home for the night."

"Oh?"

"Yes, I'm having dinner with a friend."

I gripped the phone a little tighter. This was the third weekend that she'd had plans with a *friend*. "Are you seeing someone?"

"No, I—"

"Don't lie to me, Mom!"

At my outburst, Melanie reached over and grabbed my hand in hers. Mom sighed. "Yes, I am. I've been dating a man named Bobby for a few weeks now. It's nothing serious."

I let out the breath I'd been holding in a long, exaggerated whoosh. "And why the hell didn't you think you could tell me? I mean, after all the shit that's happened, don't you believe that I want you to be happy?"

"William Thompson, watch your language!" she chided.

"Don't change the subject," I growled.

"Fine. I didn't want to tell you because my divorce isn't officially final yet. I didn't want you to think less of me, okay?"

Instantly, I felt like a giant ass. "I'm sorry, Mom. You know I could never think bad about you—you're the most amazing mom ever." I had never said a truer statement. Even though my dad had knocked her up when she was just twenty, she had never acted like she didn't want me, or that I was a burden to her life. She'd always made me feel like the most special child in the world. For the past year, we had leaned on each other to get through the nightmare that became our lives.

She sniffled into the phone. "Oh sweetheart, I appreciate you saying that."

"Well, I mean it. And please don't cry."

"I'm sorry. Are you sure you're not upset about me dating?"

"Of course not. I want you to be happy—you deserve to be happy." My comment started her waterworks again because I heard more sniffling. "Mom," I warned.

"Okay, okay, I'll stop with the crying."

"Does Dr. Leighton know you're dating?" I asked.

"Yes. She's been waiting for me to tell you."

"Great. I guess I know what I'll be discussing this afternoon in our session."

Mel squeezed my hand, and I cut my eyes from the road over to her. She gave me a sympathetic smile. "Okay, Mom, I gotta go. Mel and I are almost to Dr. Leighton's."

"I love you, sweetheart."

"I love you, too." After I hung up, I tossed the phone onto the seat beside me. "Mom's dating."

"So I heard. Are you really okay with it?"

I shrugged. "I guess so. I mean, she deserves a guy to make her happy—someone who can erase what all the asshole did to her."

"Yes, she does, and I hope this guy is the one to do it," Mel said.

"We'll see." I clenched and unclenched my jaw. "I just hate that she kept it from me."

"Maybe she wanted to wait and see how things progressed before she told you?"

"Yeah, well, I don't like the people I love keeping secrets from me. I mean, damn, I've had enough of that bullshit for a lifetime."

At my outburst, Melanie shuddered in the seat next to me. Instantly, regret filled me. I brought her hand to my lips. "I'm sorry, baby. I didn't mean it to sound like that."

"It's okay. I'm so overly emotionally lately."

"Um, it's is your period or something?"

Something about my expression amused Mel, and she busted out laughing. "No, babe, it's not PMS. It's the time of year—the almost anniversary."

I cringed when I realized we were just a few weeks away from the one year anniversary of her rape. "Oh yeah. I'm sorry."

"It's okay. Dr. Leighton thinks I might need to start coming three times a week again. Don't want to have any setbacks. Especially so close to Valentine's Day." She waggled her eyebrows.

I laughed. "I guess that means you're still down for us getting that cabin in the mountains, huh?"

"Mmm, hmm."

"Good, I'm glad to hear it," I said as I pulled into a parking spot outside of Dr. Leighton's familiar office. Just like always, I took Melanie's hand and led her inside the building.

* * *

Once our session was over and the issues of the week momentarily tackled, Mel and I headed back to the Jeep. "Ready to eat?" I asked.

"Yep, I'm starved."

"What sounds good?"

"I want to eat at Fiorenza's tonight."

My brows shot up in surprise. I wasn't used to Melanie being so certain. Usually we hemmed and hawed for a few minutes about what we wanted or where we wanted to go. "Okay, Italian it is."

We both hopped into the Jeep. When I reached for the radio, Melanie stopped me. "There's a reason why I wanted to eat at Fiorenza's."

"Oh?" I asked, cranking up.

She bobbed her head. "I asked some people to join us for dinner."

"Like JT and Lauren or some of the old crew?"

Melanie squirmed in her seat. "Um, not exactly."

"Who then?"

"Jordan Solano."

I slammed on the brakes just as I started easing out of the parking spot. My eyes widened. "Why in the hell do you want to have dinner with her?"

"Will, you know that we're friends now and how much she's meant to me."

"I know that, but it doesn't mean I have to be friends with her, does it?"

When Melanie's hopeful face fell, I felt like an epic tool. "It's just I've tried to put that part of my life behind me, Mel. I'm not going to lie that I was really stoked to hear she had moved away to Jersey. Now she's back?"

"Just for the weekend for her mom's wedding. We didn't get to see each other at Christmas. And she really wants to talk to you."

"Fucking fabulous," I muttered.

"Regardless of how it all happened, your dad took advantage of her too," Mel whispered.

Deep down, I knew that, and I should have been receptive to burying the hatchet with Jordan. From all the things I had seen and heard, Jordan had really been working on turning over a new leaf. "It's just whenever I see her, it brings back all that he did—all I'll think of is the asshole and her banging."

"Then how can you possibly look at me every day?"

I sucked in a harsh breath. Her words made me feel like I'd been kicked in the gut. "Because I *love* you. That's why I can look at you each and every day and not think of him. All I think of is how much I want to spend the rest of my life with you."

When I tore my gaze from the road, tears sparkled in Mel's eyes, but I knew they weren't sad tears. I'd learned to gage her emotions almost as well as my own. Her lips turned up in a hesitant smile. "Really?"

"Yes, really. And anytime you have doubts about me, just look down at that ring. You're not getting rid of me ever." I shook my head harshly. "You're the only one for me, Mel."

Unbuckling her seatbelt, she leaned across the seat to kiss me. "I love you so very much," she murmured against my lips.

When her tongue thrust into my mouth, I jerked back. "Hey now, I gotta watch the road."

Her hand slid from my hair to grip my thigh. "Later then," she replied with a grin.

I groaned. "Let's eat fast."

Melanie laughed. "You're so bad."

Fiorenza's was on the same side of town as Dr. Leighton's office, and we whipped into the parking lot in less than five minutes. As we swept into the foyer of Fiorenza's, I saw Jordan and some hardcore, tattooed guy waiting for us at the bar. When her dark eyes met mine, Jordan's face paled a little. It was kinda surprising to see her look so scared. She was usually such a self-assured bitch. Her attire was also a lot different. She wasn't showing off any skin or baring her cleavage. She appeared almost...pure. It was unnerving.

Melanie dropped her hand from mine before closing the gap to hug Jordan. "Sorry, I hope we didn't keep you guys waiting."

Jordan squeezed Melanie tight. "Nah, we were just catching up with the old crew. Surprisingly, even our old boss, Manny, seemed glad to see us."

Melanie giggled. "Oh yes, I remember Manny." Once she released Jordan, Melanie gave the tattooed dude a big hug as well. "Nice seeing you again, Nick." She turned around. "Will, this is Nick Deluca, Jordan's boyfriend. And Nick, this is my boy—I mean, my fiancée, Will Thompson."

With a genuine smile, Nick extended his hand. "Nice meetin' ya."

"Same to you," I replied.

"Glad to be back home again?" Melanie asked.

Wrinkling her nose, Jordan replied, "It's okay. I absolutely adore Jersey. Nick's uncle and cousins are amazing. They're like the family I never had."

"Or me either," Nick joked.

The three of them laughed, and I realized I had missed out on some important knowledge. "Can you believe my mom is actually getting remarried?" Jordan asked.

Melanie laughed. "I'm happy for her."

"After all these years, she's settling down with some boring accountant who wears glasses. Wonders never cease, huh?" Taking Melanie's hand, her gaze honed in on the sparkling diamond. "Speaking of, look at you, Miss Engaged!"

Beaming, Melanie turned back to me. "Will proposed at Christmas time. It was so romantic and beautiful under all the Christmas lights."

Jordan glanced up from the ring to smile at me. "It's gorgeous. You have really good taste."

"Thank you," I replied, tersely.

Tension hung heavy in the air. Nick cleared his throat. "Come on, Mel, why don't you and I go get us all a booth?"

"Sounds good," Melanie replied. She gave me a pleading look before following Nick to the hostess stand.

Jordan cocked her brows at me. "Wanna step outside for a minute?"

"Do you really want me to answer that question?" I asked.

Jordan sighed. "Please, Will. For Melanie?"

With a frustrated grunt, I threw open the door and stepped back out into the darkened night. When I turned around, Jordan was rubbing her arms against the cold or her nerves. "Look, I asked Melanie to dinner because I wanted to see her, but more importantly it was so I could apologize. To you."

I shoved my hands in my coat pocket. "Seriously?"

Jordan bobbed her dark head.

"Why do you even care what I think or need my forgiveness?"

"Because I do…and because I want to be able to put this all behind us." She took a tentative step

259

toward me. "In AA, they teach you to achieve true clarity and peace you need to find all those you have wronged in the past and make it right."

Okay, that's not exactly what I was expecting from her. "Since when did you become an alcoholic?"

"I didn't. Nick is a recovering addict and alcoholic."

"And he knows all about you and my dad?"

"Of course he does. He knows every deep and dirty aspect of my past. We don't have any secrets."

I crossed my arms over my chest. "I see."

Jordan's dark eyes took on a haunted look. "Will, for the last eight months, I've been working my ass off to be the person that Nick sees me as. When no one else did, he saw there was goodness within me, and I don't ever want to let him down. All I seek is redemption and repentance for my past. You're one of the last people I need to make things right with. Well, you and your mom, and I figured you would be the easier of those two."

Jesus, she actually contemplated talking to my mother? Had she lost her mind? The last person on earth my mother ever wanted to see was Jordan. I mean, she had a hard enough time looking at Melanie sometimes knowing what my dad did. Even though she's tried to get past it, sometimes Mom got an expression of both horror and disgust on her face when Melanie came over. Thankfully, it was only a fleeting moment, and so far Mel had never seen her do it. Part of me hated Mom for thinking anything negative about Melanie. I mean, she couldn't help what my dad did, and she had been shattered by him even more than Mom had.

When I glanced up at Jordan, the corners of her lips were quirked up in a small smile. It was as if she could read some of my prior thoughts. "Like I said, I just wanted to have the opportunity to say how very sorry I am that I had an affair with your father. It was selfish and stupid to do that with a man who had a wife and family."

Cocking my head, I sized her up. While the old Jordan Solano was a fake phony, everything was genuine about the girl in front of me. She truly wanted my forgiveness—she needed it desperately. And who was I to deny her? I exhaled, watching my breath fog in front of me. "Okay, Jordan, I forgive you. Or at least I'll work on forgiving you."

Her brows shot up into her hairline. "Really?"

"Yes, really. For your sake and Mel's…and I guess my own."

A beaming smile filled her face. "Oh, thank you so much, Will!" Before I could stop her, she threw her arms around me and squeezed. "I understand that it'll take time. But I appreciate you're willing to try."

"I am," I replied as I pulled away from her.

Tears glistened her dark eyes. "Not that she doesn't already know it, but Melanie's a really lucky girl."

I chuckled. "Thank you." Motioning for the door, I said, "Come on, I think we've left the loves of our lives long enough, don't you?"

She giggled. "Yes, we have."

As we swept back into the restaurant, Jordan had a definite bounce in her step. She practically sprinted to the booth where Nick and Mel sat munching on breadsticks and chatting. They both glanced up expectantly at us. Jordan and I looked at each other and smiled before sitting down. No words were really necessary to convey what had just happened. Forgiveness was about more than just words—it was actions and feelings.

As I slid into the booth next to Melanie, she leaned over and kissed my cheek. Gazing across the table, Jordan whispered into Nick's pierced ear, causing a pleased look on his face. For the rest of the evening, we didn't focus on the past. Instead, we talked about marriage, college degrees, and the restaurant Nick was going to run.

Among the four of us sitting around the booth, the past held a darkness that blotted out the sun. But the future…it was so bright.

Acknowledgements

Thanks to God for his love, support, and staying with me in the dark times.

For my students of LMS, CMS, CVHS, AMS, and CHS: Thanks for inspiring me every day of my eleven year teaching career. Your laughter, your angst, your support, your love, and your mischief made my life better. Thanks for letting me be your D*ead Poet's Society* Mr. Keating. I am forever touched and changed by each and every one of you.

To Jennifer Smalley Wood—for your unfailing support and friendship over the years. For never forgetting Nets and Lies as your "favorite" manuscript even after your initial reading three years ago. Thanks for being willing to look at its reincarnations!! In all areas of my writing career, your cheerleading, support, and optimism have meant so, so much.

To Hayley Vorholt for your Eagle Eyes and plot magic. Thanks for helping me make the story even better than I thought it could be. Your friendship and support both personally and professionally means so much to me. CF gals forever!!

To early readers Rebecca Rogers, Hannah Wylie, Rachele Mielke, and Debra Driza. Yes, it might have been years ago, but *Nets and Lies* would have never made it to this stage without you!! Big hugs and thanks for being amazing critique partners!!

To Michelle Eck for being "My Captain, My Captain" in all business savvy! But most of all for your friendship and your support!! BIG HUGS AND LOVE!!

Thanks to JB McGee for formatting help and being my master designer!! Also for your friendship.

To Cris Soriaga Hadarly for your amazing support, friendship, and love. I couldn't make it without you luvvie!!

35782971R00159

Made in the USA
Charleston, SC
18 November 2014